some may roam

a novel by
R.C. Bennett

some may roam

Distributed by:
Grove Park Publishing
Memphis, TN, USA

For all media and publication inquiries please contact
info@grovepark.us

***

This is a work of fiction. All of the characters, organizations, and events portrayed in this novel are either the product of the author's imagination or used fictitiously.

***

to my muse.

"First—if you are in love—that's a good thing—that's about the best thing that can happen to anyone. Don't let anyone make it small or light to you."

- John Steinbeck
from a letter to his son, Thom, on November 10, 1958

Chapter 1

7:00 a.m.

The quiet of the room and the warmth of the blanket held me in place while my brain made sense of the sunlight coming through the window. The sound of my alarm clock bounced off the walls and echoed through the bathroom, finally coming to rest somewhere between the carpet and the curtains.

Soft steps turned to cold tile as I made my way into the morning. The wall-to-wall mirror above the counter reflected every imperfection I'd been striving so hard to eradicate—still a little bit of love handle here, a pimple there. Nothing really, but all I could see.

Stepping down the stairs into the living room, the sound of the birds flowed in through the windows, filling the empty house. I meandered to the fridge and was greeted by a bright yellow sticky note wishing me luck and providing detailed instructions on how to warm up the breakfast that was sitting at room temperature across the counter. As was tradition, I took a precursor roll in all its lukewarm glory while the rest got warm in the microwave.

Leaning against the center island, the scent of cream cheese icing having apparently made its way to the living room, I heard Molly's footsteps round the corner into the kitchen. Not knowing much about the digestive tract of dogs other than this one's seeming capacity to consume anything that proximally mirrored food, I tossed down the last bite of hors d'oeuvre without a moment's hesitation. She licked up the fallen manna and dropped her tail to the ground, peering at the microwave as if also preparing for the properly heated main course.

Pulling out the newly warmed plate, I took a spot at the table and flipped on the TV, already set to Sports Center, Mom not having been, nor to my knowledge begun to be since, much of a TV person. Right on cue, the final commercial came to a close—something about a disease I hoped I would never get—and I had my Top Ten.

Working backward numerically, the first couple tend to be average plays that any pro could make given the opportunity to try—nothing spectacular, especially this time of year when the madness of March was nearly concluded. But with MLB rookies still stuck in the Florida sun for their extended spring training, I hoped to get a glimpse of some nineteen-year-old I'd never heard of diving into the bleachers of an empty stadium.

Number seven was a nice sliding grab over the shoulder by a college third baseman—Something State versus a directional school from I don't remember where. Then there were a couple of hockey highlights and a buzzer-beater from an NBA game mixed in before the top play—a roundhouse kick into the top shelf from some obscure beach soccer league. It was pretty impressive, but it wasn't what I was looking for.

I left the TV on but made my way to the laundry room. The pants hanging on the drying rack were still damp, but they were spotless. How Mom managed to do it, a great many scientists still wrestle. The kind of dirt that infiltrates white baseball pants is akin to the white that comes on rice. Sure, it could theoretically be separated, but it's so unlikely that we've resigned ourselves to the belief that rice is white and that white baseball pants turn brown. Or at least that is what other moms thought, sending their boys off to school with the stains of previous games still fixed across their uniform. Not Mom. I looked like a fresh set of Nike veneers every day, rain or shine.

Tossing the pants in the dryer, I turned back to the rack, pulled off my jersey, and took a good, long look at it. As a kid, the all-white uniform set was reserved for Sundays— the day when the champion of tournaments was crowned. Situated in little towns and big cities all across the country, these tournaments seemed to create their own gravitational force, requiring far too much driving, grossly underpaid umpires, and everything eleven-year-old soon-to-tear UCLs had to offer. Competing on Sunday, and winning, was a gateway drug to glory. This all-white combo was no different.

After a shower and a refresher that I, indeed, did not require a shave, I stepped down the front stoop and into the day, met by a rush of cool late-March air.

Constrained by the Mississippi River to the west and the actual state of Mississippi to the south, Memphis had grown toward the east over the years. Both Germantown and Collierville had been there, as little towns, for over a hundred years, but slowly, the line between town and city became blurred as Poplar Avenue saw buildings pop up to frame its edges all the way from Front Street to the Fayette County line. The schools emerged in a similar fashion, situated in different pockets, colored by the neighborhoods that surrounded them.

I started at mine when I was three, and while it turned out to have a pretty good academic reputation, my dad kept me there for the athletic department—small but not too small. He thought I would be able to compete without being overwhelmed. He wasn't right about much, but he turned out to be right about that. I guess the dads of all the other baseball guys had the same idea. Most of us had been there since kindergarten, so there wasn't much about each other that we *didn't* know.

The day school, where we'd started as kindergarteners, was across town, set up on the campus with the church where the school got its name. The upper school, which housed everyone from seventh grade and up, had been built much more recently and reflected the pocketbooks of the parents who stroked the tuition checks.

The sprawling campus sat on the banks of a little feeder river for the Mississippi with a bridge connecting it to Walnut Road—framed with stone walls, the school crest etched every ten yards or so on either side. It felt like you were crossing into the king's castle every morning when you came onto campus. Set down toward the right, on the dry-land side of the moat, in what I guess was really a retention pond if the river ever flooded, were four pristine grass fields, where all of the outdoor sports that didn't involve a racket or a bat practiced. To the left of the road was the middle school football field—regulation size, with little metal bleachers on either sideline.

Past all that, the road forked. To the left, the landscape opened up to reveal the field house, the high school football stadium, tennis courts, and the pool. A turn to the right, which I took that morning, led to the academic side of campus.

While underclassmen were relegated to parking near the field house, seniors got to park in the middle-school lot, which, in addition to its logistical convenience, being located much closer to the high school building and the baseball field, also served my ego quite well. As I crossed the carpool line every morning, dodging minivans and trumpet cases, I felt like the sort of hero I used to watch walk past just a few years earlier.

Even at the time, I understood that it wasn't in my *being* the best that I was arrogant—it was in my having achieved acceptance by the best. The pat on the ass always meant more than the ball landing on the other side of the fence. I was content to field one or two balls a game at third base while Sam covered the six hole with the sort of athleticism I was altogether unrelated to. I had no problem getting my B while the future ivy-leaguers at the front of the class got their A's. I was holding my own, and that's what mattered.

Sitting here now, all these years later, I guess that's why the courtroom, that first day, hit me the way it did. I knew what had gotten me there before I walked in—I had lived it. But the way I *knew* it changed—the same way a father's *knowing* changes when he holds his baby for the first time. Sure, he knew it was coming. He watched his wife's belly grow; he went to all the classes and the doctor's visits. But the way he *knew* before really had nothing to do with the way he *knows* now.

I knew of courtrooms and laws and those who had broken them. I had broken a handful of them myself, but this was something altogether unknown. I became the object of a sort of sickness you can't describe to someone who hasn't been in it. It changed the way I saw the world. It changed my place in it.

Before I ended up in here, I thought comparison was the *thief* of joy, but really, it's the comparison that makes us grateful in the first place—that helps us see the things we never noticed before. The things that we'd really like to have back. While you are living, you can't see *everything*—the living forces you to aim, and that aiming keeps you from seeing all the things outside your little tunnel. It's when you look back that you can start to piece together everything else that was lying around you, supporting you while you ran, providing shade while you rested.

So if we want to say thanks, if we want to be grateful, we do it by aiming to make more of whatever we think is good. I guess, in a way, that is what I am setting out to do here. To aim at something higher than this place, higher than the mistakes that led me here.

I know there are going to be some things that I miss, though. And that makes me scared to set out on this path in the first place. I can't tell the story of *everything* that happened that day any more than I could tell the story of *everything* that led up to that day. If you want to understand *everything* that happened, the court transcript, with all the witness' testimony, is filed away under the federal building. You can read it yourself, and you can try to understand what happened, what really happened, but expecting those facts, the words on those pages, to tell you what happened would be like trying to explain the Bellagio fountain in Vegas to some poor schmuck who just wandered into town from being stranded in the desert. It isn't so much that the fountain wouldn't make sense. It's worse than that. It's that the fountain would make all the sense in the world, but that sense would be wrong. At least wrong in the way that matters.

Chapter 2

8:15 a.m.

Holding his place as a fellow middle-of-the-packer was Doug. Not much of a ballplayer, Doug had taken the path of least resistance toward lacrosse shortly after his family moved to town the summer going into eighth grade. His dad got him a spot on a local rec team, but it didn't take long for him to realize that the baseball talent beneath the Mason-Dixon was a little more intense than wherever the hell in Indiana they'd moved from.

Physically, Doug was of average height and had above-average looks. Where either of us excelled, the other followed suit. If one of us managed to get ahead, it was pretty easy to spot a place where the other had a leg up. He beat me by a point on the ACT, but I had an inch on him in height. He pretended he wasn't jealous of my truck, and I pretended I wasn't jealous of his dad being around. Every now and then, this sort of sparring back and forth prevented us from being friends, but for the most part, it did more helping than hurting.

"You hear about Dawkins' party?" I muttered, attempting to keep my lips perfectly still as Mrs. Hyatt continued her thoughtful lecture from the front of the room.

"Yeah. He texted me about it this morning," came Doug's muffled response. Failing to pick up on the sarcasm communicated through such a hushed tone, I cocked my head toward him, to which I got one of those *"Are you fucking serious, dumbass?"* looks. Warranted, perhaps, but not at all necessary. "Of course, I haven't heard about a party at the house of a kid I've never spoken to in my life," he clarified.

While it was a small school and everyone knew everyone, everyone wasn't friends with everyone. Dawkins was a year behind us and had a rebellious streak that kept him out of the good graces of most parents, Doug's included. While Doug *was* an athlete, our orbits really only overlapped because of the AP courses. He'd become decent friends with Joe through me, but he didn't run with the baseball guys. He had his lacrosse buddies, and that was that.

As the class launched into solving some sort of problem set, Doug and I had the green light to discuss at tones much more conducive to the level of derision with which we addressed each other. "Well, his folks will be out of town again this weekend. Technically, they left yesterday, but only Biggs drinks the day before games. The rest of us are going over tonight after the game. Joe is going to get some beers if you want to come," I said in my most condescending tone, offering an invite that was far from kind but, in a sense, the most genuine a 17-year-old could offer. "I hear Britt is going to swing by," I added, just in case my invitation had come across as too sincere.

You'll get the whole story on Britt later, but suffice it to say, she wasn't *actually* invited.

"Sure," he scoffed, knowing full well that even if he wanted to blow me off, he didn't have shit else to do.

While I was decent at math in school, I was never much of a reader. I guess I never really understood why I *needed* to read. I didn't *like* reading, and I could always answer the

8

questions on the test and write the essays on the AP exams without reading the story. I was smart enough to pick up on the patterns in what the teacher said, so I guess I never looked too hard for the patterns in the books themselves. I'd just store up something a teacher or a smart classmate would say during a discussion, wait a couple of days, and then spit it back out like it was my own. I'm sure they knew what was going on, but they didn't fail me over it.

I took to reading in here, though, I guess more out of necessity than interest. At first, I'd stop by the library once a week or so. I didn't really know where to start, so it took a little while and a few quarter-read books before I found myself stuck in the stories people told of their own life. Hearing them explain the good and the bad and watching them try to make sense of the totality of what they saw, of what they'd done, what they'd left undone. It pulled at me.

Some people wrote as if they were trying to prove something, their words dripping with a neurotic precision— as if they were in a cloud, never touching the wet dirt that formed beneath their pristine little ideas. The words emerged stark white and weightless. But there were others who wrote things that seemed muddy and true. They'd crawl into the corners of my brain, coloring a new dimension into the world. Grabbing me as if they didn't exist in some *other* place—like they were somehow here and now.

Despite how much my repeated visits taught me about the Dewey Decimal system, getting my work assignment transferred was a delicate task. The sparring's not the same as it was with Doug. It's the same game—back and forth bouts establishing dominance, proving you're more useful as a friend than as a foe, that you're worth considering—but the terrain is different.

9

I saw it all pretty quickly. Dogs don't live long when they try to take over as the master of the house. But the ones who stay off the furniture, fetch the paper, and save their shit for the backyard, can live good long lives. So when I felt the time was right, I requested a transfer to the library, and it was granted.

The room itself is modest, just four walls and about a dozen shelves, but it's quiet, and there are plenty of books to have kept me busy to this point. We even have a poster hung on the wall when you come in—right there standing three feet tall with a glossy finish is the father of prison libraries himself, Mr. Stephen King. Despite the anti-establishment ending he built around Rita Haworth, his redemptive prose really moved the needle on prisons providing cons with adequate reading material.

Beneath Stephen, the door leading in faces a concrete counter that stretches the entire width of the room. Behind the counter, there's a cabinet filled with all sorts of little slips of paper: letters, poems, and the like that we call "reserved works." It's not so much that we can't take them to our cells. It's just that these works are so short—most of them aren't more than a single half page—that people could sneak off with them pretty easily if they were out on a shelf. So, they have to stay up here, but anyone who asks for them can get them. As far as I can tell, though, nobody asks for them but me.

I sit here, and I think, and I read—husbands writing to their wives, fathers writing to their sons, stuff like that. And as I read, I go to places that the cameras can't see, to anywhere beyond these walls. But no matter how far I go or how much I believe I am really *there*, I keep going back to *that* day. To *that* night and the scene of the crash.

The more I go *there*, the more I know it wasn't just her who died that day. It wasn't just the couple headed south on Walnut Road, either. That's not how things die, not in any sense that matters. There are parts of us that die with them. And there are parts of them that live—that can't be smashed by trees or pierced by windshield glass.

There's a sort of object that remains, no matter how much time passes. Because time had nothing to do with it in the first place. It's there. Whether you want to remember it or think about it doesn't change anything. And whatever *it* is, it isn't down here.

I had thought that being in here, the walls would shield me from the part of me that died, but they don't keep out as well as they keep in.

I found myself trapped in a sort of permanence I couldn't overcome. There was no way over it. And there was no way through it. I wanted so badly for the dread to get past me. I wanted to breathe, but there was nothing but fog. To say it consumed me would be to say almost nothing. It *was* me.

I knew, and it didn't so much come *to* me as it came *from within* me that I wasn't beyond having to live up to it. Beyond having to live up to *her*—to what we had. That something so beautiful and good couldn't die on its own. There were too many things resting on it, finding their place in relation to it and as a result of it. That for such a thing to be unearthed, to rot, nothing could remain the same.

Chapter 3

Louise always insisted that her brown hair was more enchanting—something about how it took just the right angle of light for it to shine. In contrast, the blonde girls apparently just walked around all day, letting their light go forth with little care as to who was on the receiving end.

But the shine that I remember, sitting here now, didn't come from her picking a table near the windows. The sort of shine that I saw in her was more like what a butterfly sees when they look at a flower. They are looking at the same thing we are when we look at flowers, but where we see red and purple and yellow and blue, they see the sorts of colors we don't even know to think about. Sure, we see the stem and the leaves and the bud. But we really don't *see* much at all. Plenty of people had the chance to see the sun bounce off Louise's hair. But they didn't see *her*. Not like I saw her.

If it is a fall that takes you into that kind of love, I think Hazel Lancaster was right, comparing it to the sort of fall that takes you to sleep. Sure, you want it to happen. Perhaps you even get enticed by how cozy the bed looks while you walk toward it, but none of those feelings really has anything to do with what it's like to be asleep or how that sort of sleep comes upon you in the first place. That sort of *knowing* is its own place, set apart from everywhere else you've ever been. Once you're there, you aren't the same as before. You don't remember leaving where you were, but you know that there isn't any going back.

However it happens, I was there. And she was there with me.

That day, though, we were also in the lunchroom, and Louise was about to take what appeared to be her third gargantuan bite of a peanut butter and jelly sandwich. Sneaking up from behind, I slipped my hands into place, yanking the back of her chair toward me, sending the front two legs up into the air, but keeping the back two nice and steady. I was careful to strike before she picked up the sandwich, though. The slice of pizza she had lost control of on my first such attempt managed to soar a full fifteen feet before introducing itself to the back of some poor freshman situated two tables over.

Her hands, unencumbered this time, flew straight to the back of my arms under my shoulders, right in that spot small enough in circumference to grab and convenient enough for a tickle. It was her favorite spot in a wrestling bout, given its tactical benefits as both a defensive and offensive position simultaneously—just what I wanted. Contact was about as hard to come by within the walls of the school as it is in here. You couldn't exactly go around making a scene in the hallway, much less in the cafeteria, but this was our little way of getting around it. She played the part of an angered damsel, and I took my role as the charming jester quite gladly.

The seat next to her was open, as it always was, but my reserved spot was only permissible because the girls knew I wouldn't stay for the whole lunch period. That and they knew I was too stubborn to give up. After about a month of my quite dramatic performances, often summoning a chair from the opposite side of the room, my customary spot became a tradition. I don't think they hated it as much as they let on—no one ever does.

After a minute or so of acknowledging my presence and sharing some generic opening remarks, the rest of the table resumed their conversation while Louise and I got to ours.

"How is the status of that curfew extension coming along?" I inquired, mustering my best corporate water-cooler-talk countenance.

"The appeal has not yet received a rejoinder," Louise declared with her chest held high as if standing before the US district attorney.

"Has Council considered a follow-up letter?"

"The great high Justice of Monroe," she started, falling out of character quite rapidly but continuing with the rhetoric, "has declared that a response is forthcoming before the first pitch of tonight's great match," as if mashing some version of Camelot with too much Law and Order.

"I like our chances," I replied, flashing a smirk that revealed a single dimple. She liked it when I did that. It was something like my version of brown hair. Only *she* got to see the dimple. "Just have Sarah take you to the game. That way, after Dawkins' party, I can drop you off at your house, and we don't have to play musical chairs with the cars. Plus, if we happen to miss curfew by a smidge, I can break out the other dimple to ease the tension with Sir Monroe."

"You know, strangely enough, I'm not sure that your little cheeks have quite the same effect on him, Mr. Crews."

"It's 2015, Madam Louise. You never know what people are into these days," I said, lifting my chin higher with each syllable, making my backpedaled exit from the table, waving royally to Louise and her compatriots.

Given the fact that fifteen years at the same institution can make even the most quality of lunch ingredients grow stale to the palette, and that I spent most of my lunch hour harassing Louise and her friends, I found the deli up Johnson Road much more suitable for a pre-game meal. We weren't "allowed" to do it, but there was an understanding of sorts that when I left, not much was made of it.

Sam and Joe shared the same sentiment. Each disembarking from their scholastic endeavors around the same time with equally weak excuses, we convened in the parking lot. Sam always drove, and the fishing poles in the backseat made the fight for shotgun all the more heated. While the poles were crammed gently up into the ceiling, the hooks dangled at varying lengths below despite our continual efforts to contain them. Sitting beneath them made me gain much more respect for the fish that manage to *not* get caught.

Sam had that sort of quiet confidence that eliminated any desire to disagree, so there was never a vote as to who drove. If he wanted to drive, you found yourself perfectly content in the backseat, hooks and all.

Standing at about six-foot-five with enough talent to earn my scholarship hitting with his eyes closed, I saved my errors for games where Sam *wasn't* pitching. Otherwise, he'd call me to the mound and chew my ass out. Where Doug and I were arrogant, Sam was just better. We portrayed it, but he *was* it. He played with a perfectionism that scared the hell out of the younger guys. I knew the feeling well. It was intimidating until it became motivating. I had caught for Sam on the 10U Memphis Tigers back in the day. He threw so damn hard that none of the other kids on the team were brave enough to get behind the dish, and most of the hitters on the other teams were too scared to get in the box. I was scared, too, but I thought the catcher's gear

15

made me look cool, so I cowboyed up. Looking back, that was probably the best baseball team I ever played on. Of the twelve guys on the roster, I know at least eight guys ended up playing college ball, a few of them for big-time programs. We qualified for the USSSA World Series at the end of the season and made it through the winners' bracket to the championship game but let the East Cobb Astros come out of the losers' bracket and beat us twice in a row to steal our trophy.

When you are that young, the travel clubs you play on have more to do with who your dad knows than how good you really are, but once you get to high school, the recruiting pressure creates a more pure meritocracy. My squad, summer going into senior year, was fine. We had a lineup full of scholarships from schools no one had ever heard of. You can still pull up the roster and see where each player was committed. The right-hand column, beside the name of each player for my roster, short one or two guys, was blank. Not because we weren't going to play college ball, but because the schools were so small, Perfect Game didn't even try to find their logos. Sam's, on the other hand, effectively served as an advertisement for the Southeastern Conference. He had a Vanderbilt logo next to his name, but we all knew he'd never step foot back on that campus as anything more than a spectator. He was set to go in the first round of the draft that summer.

All those years playing alongside him, it was an honor. I've racked my brain for a better word, a less formal word, than *honor*, but I can't find one. It wasn't just that I liked having him on my team. We were buddies, and it was nice to have the best pitcher in the district, but it was more than that. Where I had a knack for talking with the younger guys and making them feel included, Sam had a knack for going to war. I always led more like a coach, but Sam led like a fucking Navy Seal. I made sure the practices were organized and got onto the guys who showed up late or out of uniform. Sam didn't do any of that. He barely even talked to the younger guys. There was just something about the way he carried himself, though, the way he moved. He took the game so seriously that it made the whole team better. Maybe he could've done my job, but I certainly couldn't have done his. He played hard then, and he plays hard now.

Joe, on the other hand, was not first-team all-state. But he was a hell of an athlete and could play any sport with a ball. At five-foot-seven and a buck fifty, he was pound-for-pound the best football player I had ever seen. I don't know how highly he would have rated as a cover corner, but he was too slippery for pulling guards and too mean for wide receivers, so if he sniffed a run play, he'd just crash down and set the corner like an anchor in harbor, wait for the quarterback to make his move, and then drive his black-tinted visor right into the ribs of whoever was unlucky enough to be holding the ball. I watched a lot of games, and I never saw anyone get by him. Big guy, small guy, it didn't matter. They all went down the same—hard. He quit the team after sophomore year, though, because he liked duck hunting and Ole Miss football more than Saturday morning film sessions. Luckily for us, there were no major hunting conflicts with spring sports, so Joe stuck around the baseball program, although he didn't love having to miss Friday nights at Swayze.

Far stronger than his frame would lead you to believe, I didn't start out lifting Joe in the weight room until the second semester of junior year, despite outweighing him by fifty pounds. Had he been left-handed, he might have had a shot at playing college baseball, but that step and a half from the right-handed batter's box makes all the difference in the world. He played a solid center field, stole more bases

17

than anyone else at that school ever will, and the younger guys looked up to him. He was mean and tough on the field, but I'd known him as long as I'd known anybody, so I wasn't too scared of him.

Off the field, he was the same kid who, as a three-year-old, regularly showed up to preschool in cowboy boots and shorts because he was too stubborn for his mom to convince him to wear anything else. A good friend and a hell of a teammate—not the kind that goes around doling out compliments, but more the kind you'd want to have next to you in a bar fight.

My attorney showed me the video of Sam and his family when they called his name in the first round that summer. Joe was right there with him. Just like I would have been. It hit me hard then that the world was still spinning without me, but now that same memory is different. I am happy for Sam. Not happy and sad. Just happy.

Happy that he had his moment with his family and that it didn't get wrecked by me. So much during that year did, and it helps me to think about that video. Of Sam smiling with the phone to his ear and Mr. Mike trying to keep it cool while the joy seemed to be shooting out of him. A lot of work went into that moment for Sam and his folks. I know I was on his mind that day, but he got a break from it all. He had a way out. To something other than this.

Chapter 4

Following the deli, we made our way back to my house, partly out of convenience—my house being right up the road from the deli back toward the school—and partly because we knew no one was there to bother us. Or rather, no one was there to be bothered *by* us.

Dismounting from Sam's Tahoe, I backtracked toward the mailbox—a sort of hangover from the days awaiting recruiting letters. There was something in the anticipation—the walk, the heat of the black metal door flipping down, and the light gleaming off a university crest. Hope and promise in envelope form. While the correspondence was never particularly abundant, it was non-existent now, considering my letter of intent was binding, at least for the first year.

As I followed Sam and Joe, the garage door was already on its way up. The code, while not difficult to remember considering it was printed across the front of the house, was a stumper for my buddies for a long while after we first started driving. Around that time, my house turned into a sort of afternoon respite. Getting in, on the occasions when Sam or Joe beat me home and Mom was still at work, started as a necessity but quickly became a sort of game where they would try and surprise my mom, sitting in the living room or pretending to make an evening meal upon her return from work.

There was something pure about those days. Like the morning is pure. We went there to prepare, not to escape. We could relax, play video games, and get ready for night games in peace. The belonging that came with those days, that of all the houses, my house became the landing spot, sticks out like the first clover in spring, shooting up above the dead grass all around it.

It wasn't the kind of house that Dawkins had, and that's not a knock on Dawkins' folks. They were kind, warm people. Maybe they should have known what was going on at the house when they left, or maybe they did know and should have cared. Maybe they thought that the drinking and the partying was just what high school kids were supposed to do for fun. It's not like we would have done things any differently if they hadn't left town so much. We would have just gone to some other spot. We never got caught, but that really only happens at the sort of house where no one is trying to catch you.

Deep down, we wanted to pretend we were adults, and that was the only way we knew how to do it.

Dawkins, in his own right, wasn't a bad kid. He had a tough combo of dyslexia and attention deficit disorder, so he struggled academically. He'd do anything for you, but he had a tough time following rules. Even when we were little, though, the teachers knew he had a keen eye for where the real line was. And he never crossed it. So when they got onto him, it was only out of principle, never anger. He got held back in the first grade due to the "learning disabilities," but personally, I think it was a croc of shit. Dawkins was always plenty smart. He just didn't read as fast as the rest of us. And if he couldn't concentrate, it was because that damn personality of his couldn't be confined to the silly exercises they make you do in grade school.

By the time we got to high school, though, he had learned to play the game. He showed up to class, kept his mouth shut, turned his homework in on time, and if he needed to, he'd beg teachers for a C at the end of the semester. What he lacked in book smarts, he more than made up for with his ability to negotiate.

On the diamond, he was a utility guy, filling in the hole of whoever was pitching that day. He wasn't much of a shortstop, but Sam got about half his outs by strikeout, so it was alright that the left side of the infield was less than stellar on the nights that Dawkins and I had to cover it ourselves. Being a grade behind us and finding himself under constant administrative scrutiny, Dawkins wasn't allowed to leave school early, even on game days. Doug would swing by my house occasionally as our resident outsider, but most afternoons, in the spring at least, it was just me, Sam, and Joe.

Doug had been steering clear of Mom around that time anyway, as the sting of my first run-in with the law had not entirely worn off. And while it wasn't Doug's fault, per se, his involvement landed him at least partial guilt within Mom's court of law.

I guess the run-in really started two years prior to senior year, with our collective loss of baby fat toward the end of tenth grade. I was busy chasing Louise while Doug's newfound physique was starting to garner the attention of more girls than he knew what to do with. Lacking the requisite vision to discern logically, Doug stumbled blindly into a relationship that might as well have taken place on the moon. He thought that since Brittney was a year older and "*cooler*," he was above hanging out with Joe and me, so we didn't hear from him outside of school hours for almost an entire year until the whole thing blew up.

When it did, I could tell he was in a bad spot; falling to the earth all the way from the moon leaves a mark. They tried the whole long-distance thing, but Virginia is a long way from our side of Tennessee. From the way he told it to me, there was no fight in her voice. She didn't even seem to care that he cared. It was a pretty tough hand to be dealt, so despite his abandoning us for the majority of the relationship, Joe and I figured we'd do the same thing he'd do for us. We got together as many beers as we could and found a spot where we could exorcize his broken-hearted demons.

The problem with drinking, especially when you're seventeen, isn't so much that you have bad ideas. It's that you have really good ideas which happen to completely disregard the likelihood that anything could go wrong. The particular good idea we had that night involved taking our liquid courage with us to get some late-night batting practice up at the school. Despite Doug's inability to compete in the southern travel-ball circuits, he knew enough about the game to at least enjoy some late-night shenanigans.

We piled into my truck and covered the short commute from Joe's place to campus, finding a spot close to the field, but not so close as to raise suspicion. We made our way under the cover of darkness toward the indoor facility, case of beer in tow. Joe punched in the code, flipped on the lights, and we were ready to rumble.

After emptying every bucket and cart the place had to offer, we figured enough was enough. Doug seemed to have gotten some of his sadness out. He tried to pretend it was anger, but when you get treated the way he was, there's no anger. Not yet, at least. I could tell he was sad, but he seemed a little less sad by the time we were done.

We packed up all the beers, flipped off the lights, and made our way back to the truck. There was no sign of the security officer; we were up and out of there without a hitch. I hung a left and then the first right before the left-ward slide of my truck jammed into my memory that Joe's neighborhood wasn't the first right—it was the second.

With little by way of street lights and my fine motor skills sufficiently dulled, I had managed to turn us right into an undeveloped patch of mud. It wasn't pretty. None of us had permission to be out at this hour in the first place, and everyone's parents thought they were at some other place, none of which were that field. And *that field* is where we were stuck, considering my two-wheel drive was all hat and absolutely no cattle.

After a minute or so of sheer panic, I managed to regain some semblance of control and strung a couple thoughts together. I knew the owner of the subdivision; his kids went to our school, a few grades behind us, so I figured he wouldn't be too bent out of shape by a few idiots getting their truck stuck in his field. If we could get out and make our way back to Joe's, we could find a way to piece together a less-incriminating timeline and take our reprimanding without handcuffs.

My scheming came to an abrupt halt, though, when that unmistakable shade of blue lit up all that had transpired. Mud-footed and by any measure over the legal limit, we were pinched in.

Doug was inconsolable. Whatever defenses he had were no match for all of this. There was no self-preservation. No resolve. He melted. Falling down into the mud, he broke.

For his part, the officer read the room. Except for the not-yet-completed patch where I had landed, the rest of the subdivision had been finished, filled with sleeping suburbanites. It was dead quiet. No one needed to be alerted. It didn't affect anyone else, and we certainly weren't going to make a run for it. We were cuffed, and the officer sat us up on the bed of my truck while we waited for another squad car to take us to jail. Doug was still a mess, but Joe's posture on the other side of him kept me upright.

Every minute felt like an hour, but even I knew we hadn't been in the holding cell for long when an officer came in and told us we could make a phone call. There was no escaping the fact that our parents would find out, and I felt pretty sure the school would piece together that we'd been on campus. But the clock outside the holding cell read four a.m., so I thought there might be time to at least get out of there and break the news to my mom without the backdrop of squad cars and cinder block walls. Joe got on the phone and called Coach.

Being the early bird we were counting on him to be, Coach picked up on the second ring. The fact that his son wasn't a stranger to making the same call might have aided in his picking up a random number. Hell, he might've had it saved. Either way, he came and got us, posted our bail, and took us back to Joe's. I doubt Joe and Doug's bail was much of a concern, but mine couldn't have been cheap. I never asked, and he never brought it up.

About thirty minutes into blank, hungover stares into nothingness, the buzz of my phone jolted us back to life. It was Coach. Long story short, the guy who donated the money for the new indoor batting facility was an attorney. When Coach told him that a couple of guys *may or may not have* run into some trouble after they *may or may not have* been in the indoor facility, our benefactor decided it would be best if the whole thing went away. He assured Coach that he'd make some calls. Considering that the Winchesters, who owned the land where the cops had left my truck, knew us and wouldn't have any desire to press charges over us rearranging some mud, he thought the whole thing could get dropped.

I didn't know, and am still unsure, how such things get "dropped." I had always thought of the justice system as a sort of vending machine, where once the button is pressed, you can put money in for something else, but there's no going back on the first request. Turns out, my notion wasn't entirely wrong. But Coach said to sit tight and not say anything yet. The pounding in my chest rattled my hands so much that I had to set my phone down on the deck whenever Coach called so that Joe and Doug wouldn't see my nerves.

All of this hurts to put down now. We thought we had avoided the consequences altogether, and were wiser for it. I guess it would be easy to stop the story and start the race of pointing fingers. I had done more than enough to warrant any that managed to be pointed in my direction, but I don't think I can blame Coach for trying to help. It would be easy to say that he and everybody else were just covering their own asses, and maybe they were, but if that's true, it's not the whole truth. They saw themselves in us. They had done the same sort of shit we were doing, and they'd managed to turn themselves into something.

No one had really thought through the ramifications of giving teenagers unrestricted access to an enclosed space without any sort of video monitoring. Or if they had, we had acted too quickly for them to even implement their plans. The building was still so new that we just called it "The

Indoor" since they hadn't put up the sign with the guy's name who donated the money.

We can argue about who should have done what and how it could have been handled, but that's how it went down. I was driving the truck. The officer knew it. I knew it. I didn't tell Coach in so many words, but he understood the implications of my bail being higher than the others. Mr. Winchester knew no one would bother him over a couple of minor-in-possession charges. No one had to tell anybody. Everyone knew exactly what had gone down.

And once that sort of genie starts swirling, it's not going back in the bottle. You may never see it again, and the dice may fall your way long enough to where you feel it's behind you, but the truth has a way of *being* no matter how much the memory of it fades.

Chapter 5

Despite, or perhaps as a result of, Doug's absence, the afternoon was going exactly as planned. I was up 2-1 on the pool table and had split 1-1 in The Show. The circular imprint Sam had wedged into the ceiling with his pool cue added to the running tally of similar frustrations.

Mom had meticulously measured the room to ensure we could play pool without breaking any windows or smashing her walls, but she hadn't considered the distance between the end of a cue and the ceiling, especially in the hands of someone whose center of gravity was about as tall as she is. I'd put a few holes in the ceiling, too, but most of them were Sam's. I think Joe might've made one just to show that his height didn't affect his ability to compete at our level of dumb-assery. Either way, we'd managed to kill most of the time between lunch and our five-thirty curtain call. We headed down the stairs and made our way back to the parking lot. This time, Joe was stuck with the hooks.

Sam, not even thinking about allowing his truck to come to a complete stop, slowed down just long enough for Joe and me to hop out. Making my way over to my truck, I pulled back the sunburnt handle. It was one of those early spring days where it's not too hot for the oven of a parked car to annoy you yet. I sat down, leaving the door open but letting the pinned-up heat wash over me, feeling the veins in my arms come toward the surface.

Peering through the windshield, the lot was packed. Students streamed out, eager to head home, while the parents of the junior varsity squad rushed in, having left work early to make the four o'clock game. The game hadn't started yet, but I could see Coach Clarke standing at home plate across from the JV coach for the other team.

Coach Clarke was a good guy—is a good guy, I guess. He was the first coach to tell me to *try* to hit a home run. Normally, coaches don't give that advice. They say something dumb like, "Now just try and hit something hard for me here, Crews." Not Coach Clarke. During a JV game sophomore year, I remember he called me down the third base line during a pitching change, held his finger up in the air, and said, "You feel that, Crews?"

It's one of those memories, even now, where I can almost plop myself right back into it, feel the grass under my spikes, and see everything just the way it was that day.

With a grin sneaking up toward my ear, I chimed back, "Wind's blowing out dead to left field," my shoulders seeming to jolt upward with every syllable.

"You're damn right it is. What do you say you try and get something up in the air? See what happens. Hell, you may be able to get one out of here."

I nodded, trying to contain my zeal, and made my way slowly back toward the plate. Flipping the bat over to my left hand, the end pointing straight to the sky, I took in a breath, letting it out all at once right as the last warm-up pitch made its way into the catcher's mitt.

I stepped toward the box, and squatting toward the dirt, I got a good lather for both hands, rubbed them together, and took a look at the pitcher, who was looking right back at me. Standing up, I brought my right foot into the box, just a smidge in front of the back chalk. With a slight wiggle, I found a good resting place for it. Holding my right hand up toward the umpire, I reached out with my left and tapped the far side of the plate with the bat before drawing it back inward, tapping the inside edge of the plate. Maintaining a fluid motion, I wheeled the bat until its end was aimed directly at the pitcher. Lowering my back hand, I released the breath that had come into the box with me, adjusting my cup in the process. In a smooth sort of rhythm, I brought my hands together, right hand finding its place atop left, pinched my elbows together just a touch as I slid my hands back in a mimic of my loading position.

Finally, I dropped the handle of the bat to my shoulder. I'd watched Josh Hamilton do the same thing during the World Series where they lost to the Cardinals. I thought it was intimidating that he just stood there, bat on his shoulder, staring at the pitcher like he didn't have a care in the world. I had all the cares in the world. I ate, slept, and breathed baseball, but I figured if I dropped my bat to my shoulder, I would look laid back. Not sure if it worked or if my version of the Matt Carpenter lean, where I basically showed my package to every fan sitting down the fist base line, added to the mystique. But I did both. Every time.

There were a couple of pitches to start the at-bat—maybe a foul ball and one or two way out of the zone. Sometimes new pitchers have the jitters, so it takes them a minute to rein it in. That time, though, I didn't give him much time to get comfortable. He put one in the middle of the zone, just above knee height, and I got every single piece of it. The center field wall read "385" in bright yellow letters beneath a batter's eye about twenty feet tall. The ball cleared all of it. I didn't know what to do with myself. I'd hit some home runs growing up on tiny fields, but this was the real deal. I didn't know I could hit a ball that far.

Everyone there, if they were watching at all, just saw a three-run home run amid a seemingly inconsequential game. They saw me celebrating like an idiot, too, I suppose, but they had no idea what that ball flying over that batter's eye meant.

Freshman year, I might as well have been trying to make the cheer squad. There was no way I could have gotten on the field. We had a division-one scholarship at every spot, with the only exception being Biggs behind the plate. He started as a true freshman but gave up his hopes of playing college ball because one single coach from one single SEC school said he was too short to play at the next level. I think that's why he started drinking the night before games. He figured he might not be tall enough to play at UT, but he was good enough to be the best catcher in the district, hungover.

But me, I didn't even have a varsity jersey as a Freshman. I wore number thirty-nine, which was noticeably absent in the uniform set the varsity team wore. Didn't matter to me, I watched their games from the stands. When they went on the road, they didn't bother taking the JV.

Sophomore year, though, those guys were gone, and with Sam moving from third base to shortstop, I figured I had my chance. Incorrect. The last week of February practice, I was informed that while the varsity team was headed to the beach for a spring break tournament to start the year, I was staying with the JV on a tour of every podunk town along Highway 51, right here in beautiful West Tennessee. We'd meet up with the varsity team for the Saturday game once they were back from the beach.

It was *that* Saturday game, with the wind blowing out dead to left field, that I got every piece of that ball. No one had ever hit a home run in a JV game that I had ever seen. Guys with that kind of pop played varsity. I figured Coach would have to call me up.

Instead, I spent the rest of the month feeling sorry for myself at the four o'clock games with Coach Clarke. Despite my bad attitude, I was in the sort of zone I had never been in before at the plate. I knew I was better than every guy I faced, *and I was.* I don't know if Coach left me down there on purpose or what, but I had to go damn near two straight weeks without getting out a single time and hit three more home runs before he finally gave me a start on varsity, just in time for region play.

All of that flooded back, sitting there in the baking heat of my truck, looking at Coach Clarke. I didn't skip the JV games like Joe and Sam did. I wanted the JV guys to know they were part of the same team as me. I had worn the same JV uniform, and I knew what it was like to play the four o'clock game. Nobody but your parents in the crowd, the sun beating down the first base line because it hadn't had time to set. No walkup music, no hype. Just two B-teams getting after it before the real action started.

The buzz of my phone distracted me from the field. A blurry photo taken from what appeared to be the front door of the high school—barely recognizable as me. Louise knew I would be sitting right here, and I knew she'd text me. There wasn't a whole lot of time between when she left school, as part of the rule-following tribe, and her four o'clock swim practice, so we had to time our virtual philandering quite precisely. Her blurry photo said, *I see you out there. Go get 'em.*

31

I responded with a simple *;)*, figuring it smoothest to keep my cards close to the vest.

<3 came the response, and our haiku was complete.

I held down the power button, shutting down my phone, and tossed it in the console before heading toward The Indoor. Acknowledging the mural of my face and those of the other senior players on the way in, I set down my bag but brought my glove and helmet with me as I made my way back toward the dugout. Barely looking a day over thirteen, Harris, a freshman lefty, was finishing up his pre-game routine on the bullpen mound. I gave him a nice pat on the ass and meant it.

I walked through the gate closest to the dugout and made my way toward the helmet rack. Since the varsity and JV shared the same dugout, varsity guys were supposed to keep their helmets in The Indoor until the JV game was over. I put mine on the rack. Licking my finger to clear a smudge of dirt off the back lettering, I revealed a crisp 28, my varsity number. By this time, Coach Clarke was standing at the railing, deep in conversation. I leaned toward him, giving the top of his shoulders a gentle squeeze. He cocked his head toward me without missing a note of the advice he was imparting to the young freshman.

I found a nice place on the top row of the bench and placed my glove eloquently so as to keep the shape in perfect position. Back against the cinderblock wall, I pulled my Oakleys down from my hat, slid them on, and took in the scene. Coach was dragging the infield one last time. Crisp, white chalk lines ran from the edge of the infield grass out toward the outfield on either side of view. A freshman, Judson Smith, standing about five-foot-four with a jersey so big that his number was about halfway tucked into his pants, made his way toward the second-base plug with a fresh white base in hand. Setting it into position, he made his way carefully back toward the infield grass. Coach swung around, pulling the drag between the base and the lip, covering the last set of tracks left on the dirt. It was pristine.

The players, moving in a swarm around the dugout, began filing down to meet Coach Stephens in shallow right field. After a minute or so, I got up and made my way as well. Jersey flapping majestically in the wind, I slowly found my position next to him. The players lined up along the foul line, and I took my spot as the pretend pitcher, sometimes making my move toward home plate and sometimes flipping my hips, sending all the players back toward the foul line. Inevitably, one or two would misread the situation and take off in the wrong direction. Coach Stephens would jog over and offer his words of wisdom while I kept running everyone else through the drill. After a few minutes and more successful pickoffs than Coach Stephens hoped I would make, he sent the players back to the dugout.

There is this tendency that pulled at me, and I am sure it pulled at the coaches, too, to focus all my attention on the guys like Sam. Making sure they approved of the way I played. Going out of my way to make it clear to the younger guys that I was friends with the guys who had real talent. That they approved of me. As if that would earn me respect. But Coach Stephens had earned a different kind of respect. We knew he cared. We had plenty of coaches who cycled through the program that just wanted to say they knew a major leaguer. I could tell that Coach Stephens wasn't that way, though, and I tried to do the same. His patience for the kids without a lick of talent told me everything I needed to know.

If you looked at his players or the JV record, you might think that he and Coach Clarke weren't worth much. And I guess, in a sense, you'd be right. But that would be like saying I hated JV ball. If I hadn't wanted off that JV team so bad during my sophomore year, I wouldn't have been out there running pre-game drills *that* day. The JV game would've just been water coming out of a nozzle to me. I wouldn't have seen the fountain. It would have just been one B-team playing another B-team. But it wasn't that to me at all. And it wasn't just that these guys were future varsity players, either. Plenty of them would only earn ceremonial letters, not ones based on innings played. It was something deeper.

I don't know why those pre-game warmups mattered so much to me, but I *do* know that those guys hung around for the varsity games. They were in the dugout right next to us, while I had been in the stands a few years earlier. When we went on the road, they came with us. I don't know if it was the fact that they knew I spent a year and a half in their uniform, or if they knew how proud I was to have moved beyond their uniform into a varsity set. Those sorts of things live in a way that you can't put your finger on. They are a million little things all at once. You don't know how they come together or really what they are now, but they are more real than anything you can touch.

That's what my life was. It was a million little details from a million little decisions. Some good, some not-so-good, but it was mine. Or at least I had my place in it. And when you fuck that up. When that slams into oncoming traffic at two in the morning, there's nothing left. There's nothing that stays the same. There's no flowing jersey. There's no pre-game drills. There's no glimmer in the eye of the freshman who looks up to you. There's none of that.

There is just what happened.

Chapter 6

4:30 p.m.

I keyed in the entry code and stepped back onto the turf of The Indoor. The smell of fresh rubber was still so strong it went straight past my nose and drilled the back of my head. It was quiet. Nobody there yet to warm up for the varsity game, and all the JV guys in the dugout for their own game, it was the next step in my pregame ritual. The younger guys knew the drill—they left the place tidy, not a single ball out of place. The buckets and carts were filled to the brim, and they had even left my tee right where they knew I'd want it: left-hand cage, middle of the zone, about two baseballs beyond the front edge of the plate.

The Indoor was pretty big, stretching about a hundred or so feet in length and slightly less than half that in width. Two long cages ran parallel, with about ten feet of space between them. The netting was soft, so there was some give when you hit into them. Strung up on cables, we could slide them back and turn the room into something like half an infield.

After the place opened, Coach had us hang a net dividing the right-side cage in half, so more guys could get work in at the same time. But we kept the left-side cage open, extending about seventy feet or so. Long enough to take live at-bats in.

If you wanted to hit off a tee, which most guys didn't, you were supposed to hit in between the cages, back toward one of the nets, or at least in the right-side cage. The left-side cage was reserved for Coach to throw pregame batting practice, but since I got there before anyone else, I could hit wherever I damn well pleased.

I needed to see the ball travel. I needed the feeling of putting one right in the corner of the netting, making the bearings jump off the tracks, banging back down in a visceral thud.

After picking a tune off the communal iPod and tinkering with the frayed aux cord, aligning it just right, the surround sound was up and running. Wood bat, Voodoo, and drop-ten Stealth in tow, I pulled up the corner of the netting, dipped my head under, and fell into Zen.

First came a few swings with the wood bat, getting my feel for the middle of the barrel. I had a couple thuds before the first beloved *thwack* rang off the walls and into my veins. Everyone has a different opinion about switching back and forth between wood bats and metal bats mid season. I always found that the sweet spot on wood bats was just a little bit farther up the barrel than on a metal bat, which threw some guys off, but there was no disputing that the sweet spot was smaller on wood bats. Warming up, even if it was just a dozen or so swings with the wood bat, feeling the unmistakable nothingness of the bat meeting the ball with more punch than the ball had to offer in return, it made me feel like swinging a metal bat was easy.

After popping the back of the cage four times in a row, I dropped the wood bat and picked up the Stealth—black with green letters and a green composite handle. It looked like a toothpick compared to my other bats, so in addition to the calm its sentimental value brought me, having been my weapon of choice as a 10-year-old Tiger, the weight made it perfect for my single-hand drills. Three in a row off the back net with the bottom hand, three in a row off the back net with the top hand, and on I went, working both hands out beyond the edge of the plate and then back to the middle of the zone, stretching the tee up to its tallest position. Laser after laser. I was dialed in.

I flipped to the Voodoo—midnight black with a sinister-looking piece of white artwork wrapped around the barrel, its appearance matched its name. Thirty-three inches long and thirty ounces in weight, I'd swung it off and on since sophomore year despite Demarini issuing new models every season. I was partial to this one. Tee back in its starting position just beyond the front edge of the plate, the bearings holding up the net slammed, ball after ball, over and over. A symphony.

With both tiers of the modified shopping cart empty, I made my way toward the chair set up for me in the corner of the cage and took a rest. Back slouched, my gaze found the upper corner of the cinder block wall. Fresh black paint stopped on a dime as the turn of the architecture made way for a smooth, cream ceiling. I surveyed the entirety of the edge, from wall to wall, before closing my eyes and taking a long breath.

The music was loud, but I could hear myself think. No single thread of cognition, just a million free radicals swirling and dashing. The smirk I could feel starting to form drove my left eye open just enough for me to see the tiny black heart Sharpied onto a tattered, dirt-brown Evo-shield as my hands made their way to the top of my head. No more than a quarter of an inch across, the little piece of art was her way of coming onto the field with me.

The first one she'd ever drawn came on our first real date. I'd already signed for the check but needed to release the seven waters I had nervously drowned during the evening's meal before driving her home. As I made my way back from the men's room, Louise slid out of the booth, knocking the pen—that the waitress had left atop the check—onto the floor in the process.

I paused for a second, noticing her face turn bright red, wondering if she'd ignored me fumbling over myself all night. Somehow, though, through the haze of hormones and adolescent idiocracy, I managed to put two and two together. In reaching down to pick up the pen, I noticed the receipt had moved, ever so slightly, from where I'd left it. And I noticed something else. There was a tiny, almost indistinguishable heart, not on the copy I'd signed but on the one underneath—the one you can take with you, but nobody born after 1970 does. I didn't know if she thought I'd see it later or if she just drew it for herself, but I could tell in that moment that whatever her intentions, she had not planned on me seeing it right then.

She dropped her eyes and slid past me toward the door. Her escape would be short-lived, considering I was her ride home, and I was holding the chicken tenders she'd promised to bring home to her brothers, but I gave her a couple steps head start so she could pull her thoughts together.

I dropped the pen back on the table and folded up the customer copy nice and neat before securing it in the pocket of my jacket. The head start wasn't just for her. A golden opportunity had fallen into my lap, but there wasn't much time to determine what to make of it.

Hands tucked firmly into the front pockets of her jeans, partially out of nervousness and partially because she was short a jacket on a night where one was definitely required, Louise made her way down the sidewalk in front of me. Her cropped sweater, stopping just above the waist of her jeans, gave way to a view that was far from hard on the eyes.

Tilting my head side to side, "I regret it," came my opening remark. I pulled the receipt from my pocket and lifted it through the silent air toward the fluorescent lighting of the covered walkway, casting a shadow of my silhouette onto the concrete just to the right of her. Her headband dipped out of sight as her chin tucked toward her chest. Not side to side in anger. Straight down in defeat, as if crushed. I watched her try and reclaim her voice before mounting a response.

"I..," she started before I cut her off.

"The Smokey Melt was shortsighted," I said, my pomp in full swing, continuing as if I was oblivious to her lack of composure. "It's not that it isn't good. It's delicious. We had a tough practice today, so I earned a little bit of greasy goodness, and I knew that you were going to go with the tenders. We'd already discussed it. But something just changed when you actually ordered them. All of a sudden, I knew I was making a mistake."

The heel of her white Reebok drove into the sidewalk as her left shoulder dropped toward me, initiating a turn. I took a gamble that she'd want me to keep stride as her spin eliminated the distance between us. Neither of us moving in reverse, I could feel her heart beat. Eyes locked, she pulled her fist back slowly and whispered, "You weren't supposed to see that," before delivering the softest punch I'd ever received and spinning right back around from where she came.

"What do you mean, *see that*?" I yelled as if she was a mile away. "I was sitting right there when you ordered."

No response.

I followed her to the truck and settled into the driver seat, dutifully positioning my newfound artwork into place on the underside of the sun visor. Bringing my left hand up to the wheel, I looked off as if into a great expanse and gave it a minute as her eyes burned a hole into my cheek. Then, still facing forward, I started my sentence, but this time *she* cut *me* off.

"I like you," she blurted as if the words were shot out of her mouth with gunpowder. Then, more softly, she continued, "I like you, Crews. I was nervous to say yes to this date because I already knew that I liked you."

"Seems like a strange reason to be nervous."

A stare. No response. Just a stare. A quiet resolve in her eye. She fucking meant it.

"Well, obviously, I like you. I don't buy chicken tenders for Dawkins when I bring him to Hueys," came my witty yet not entirely unromantic reply.

Her face went red, but not the same shade as before. She came down off the side of her seat and fell back into the chair, arranging her hand on the center console next to mine, her eyes staring straight into the non-existent horizon. The black nail polish, which had been fresh about an hour earlier, was picked to oblivion. I took the hint, moving my hand onto hers. They were soft and warm. And I was hooked.

Chapter 7

sometime between 4:30 and 5:00 p.m.

As my eyes opened, I noticed the aux cord must've lost its delicate positioning. The music had stopped, but I wasn't sure for how long. Nothing but the occasional ping of a bat or thud of a glove, muffled by the hardness of the thick cinder block walls, made its way to my ears. I closed my eyes again.

The memory of my driver's license still wet from the DMV printer emerged from the cloud of thoughts. A 3-2 win to open region play, I was officially a varsity player. I stifled a drag-bunt attempt in the first, made an over-the-shoulder grab on a foul ball in the fourth, and drove in the tying run in the sixth with a sac fly. They weren't going to mention me in the paper, but I had held my own.

The day before, I was a B-teamer who hung around the concession stand after practice, waiting for a ride home from my mom. But that day, I was the starting third baseman on a winning team with a set of keys to anywhere I wanted to go sitting in my locker.

As I jogged out to the right field fence, we received a warm welcome from a student section that was primed from the bootlegging that *may or may not have* taken place in the cozy outfield hideaway. It was my first time participating in the post-game tradition.

Sticking out like a sore thumb, I found Caleb, a behemoth of a man, even at sixteen years old, manning the grill. He'd played with us freshman year and was a real ballplayer, but he left the team in the offseason to focus on football. His dad, somehow even larger, had been an All-American at Auburn in the eighties, and Caleb's older brother had just finished his second season playing for Dan Mullen down at Mississippi State. Not too much of a socialite, I knew Caleb worked the grill so he didn't have to make small talk. While everyone else was there to catch a weekday buzz or to just be a part of the crowd, Caleb watched the game. He handed me a cold, charred hotdog embellished with perfectly straight lines of mustard and ketchup and a dollop of horseradish. I received it with a grin and looked up to him, waiting for his post-game analysis.

I don't remember what he said, but I remember what he meant. He knew how hard I had worked. He knew what it was like to play JV ball. He knew what it was like to come off the bench as a pinch-hitter. Weight of the world on your shoulders. No chance to find the rhythm. Just dropped in during the middle of the chorus, expected to find the beat. He knew all of it, so I knew what that hotdog meant. I hated horseradish, but not that night.

Hands sticky from condiments but wary of mixing mustard stains with my hard-earned dirt stains, I wiped myself off with the Dri-FIT I had on underneath my jersey. We had a weird color, my high school, that was tough to match. Pretty similar to Florida State, we weren't red, but we weren't maroon either. So, finding sleeves to match our uniform was a daunting task. Most guys just ended up landing on black, but I couldn't accept that. I'd tried every shade of red the internet had to offer, finally terminating my quest with a set of Nike sleeves from a volleyball equipment website. I trimmed them to a perfect three-quarter length and wore them every game, which served my superstition nicely but left the garment with an odor that no washing machine could eradicate.

I saw Louise on the first tier of the makeshift deck we'd constructed during the offseason, and suddenly I actually felt concerned that our lack of measuring and overall lackadaisicalness might not be safe. *"Eh, no one has fallen yet,"* I reassured myself as I made my way, meandering thoughtfully over to where she was standing, hoping that the smell of my Dri-FIT would be indistinguishable amongst the overall odor of the team.

As coordinated, my wingman, Sarah, was in place right next to her. Neighbors for their whole life, Sarah and Dawkins were that sort of couple that didn't have to hold hands for you to know they were together. Where Dawkins' personality filled the room, Sarah's made it feel small and intimate. She moved through life with a sort of playfulness that made every interaction an adventure. I think there was a part of Dawkins that would have never made it to the surface if it weren't for Sarah, and there was a part of her that was more free because of him. Despite being four months younger than Dawkins, her reading comprehension skills kept her from being held back, so she stayed in my class as we worked through grade school, leaving Dawkins a class behind—the same class as Louise.

That all matters because every new student at our school got what the faculty calls a *buddy*. The idea is that the buddy helps make the new kid feel comfortable and gives them a head start at making friends. Normally, you get someone in your own grade, but I guess because Sarah was friends with so many of the girls in the class behind her, the school just forgot which grade she was actually in and assigned her to be Louise's *buddy*. Whatever the reason, it worked out well

44

for me because not only did Sarah date one of my teammates, she could drive. She knew I was going to make my approach after the game—assuming we won and I didn't suck—and she knew I'd need her to give Louise a ride to Huey's for the post-game meal.

In preparation for the night, Sarah had filled me in on the basics. Born in May of '98 while her dad was stationed at Fort Stewart, Mary Louise Monroe stood about five-foot-five and swam the hundred-meter freestyle. I had been unaware our school had a swim team, but she gave me a newfound reason to learn about such things. I wasn't quite sure how someone so small could swim so fast, but I took Sarah's word for it. I also learned from Sarah that Louise's dad flew air support for the Marines during the Gulf War. A West Point grad with a ranger tab, "nice guy" did not seem fitting despite Sarah's characterization of him as such. I didn't know much about the military, but I knew that nice guys don't fly Apaches. Raised all over the place, Louise's family settled just outside of Dallas about the time her youngest brother was born. Her dad eventually made the switch to civilian life, but the lack of bullets flying didn't make his absence from home much easier, or his international flights any quicker. In the summer of 2012, he moved Louise and the rest of the family to Memphis, finally managing to get a job in aviation that allowed him to stay in one place. All in all, despite not being a Texan by birth, Louise seemed to be plenty Texas for me.

I could tell Louise was saying something to Sarah, but Sarah was distracted by the incoming romance. "Y'all coming to Huey's?" I yelled, making sure to include Louise with obvious disregard for the fact that we'd yet to speak a single word to one another. The hallway eye contact had boiled to the point that something needed to be said, but I felt an indirect approach would be tactically superior.

"Huey's?" Louise replied softly, but more at Sarah than at me.

"You've lived here eight months, and you haven't been to Huey's?" I spouted. Turning to address Sarah, the thought immediately thrust to the front of my mind that I was not supposed to know that she'd only lived here for eight months. I crammed the fear backward and brought up some humor to remedy my misstep, "What kind of operation are we running here, Sarah?" I added, confidence not missing a beat.

"You know there are more places to eat, Crews?" Sarah remarked in a sort of question that leaned more toward condescension than curiosity.

"Really, I'll believe it when I see it."

"When are y'all going?" Louise said, this time looking at me.

"Uhhh, now-ish?" I replied with genuine ambiguity.

"We could be convinced," Sarah chimed as if the whole thing weren't scripted.

"I'll come," Louise said, piercing straight through the charade with a sort of sincerity that I wasn't ready for, "but I need to take my brothers home first."

Looking around, I noticed two kids that did, upon a more thorough examination, seem out of place amongst the sea of highschoolers—minding their own business, throwing a lacrosse ball back and forth in complete disregard for the evening's entertainment. I figured they must be her little brothers.

"I'll bring her," Sarah added affectionately as she moved down the rickety deck and toward the parking lot. I gave a wave and turned back toward the infield.

Despite my promotion to varsity and place in the right-field fan festival, as a sophomore, I still had post-game field duties. We raked the cutouts around third base and first base while Coach drug the rest of the infield, a handful of guys tamped the mound, and Biggs supervised the other catchers while they repaired the dirt around home plate. We were less than thorough, but eventually, Coach gave the thumbs up that we were good to go. Dawkins and I backtracked to The Indoor to get Joe, who, as an outfielder, managed to escape all field duties, before piling into my truck and making our way, in a combined odor, up the road to Huey's.

After what seemed like a decade, the door finally cracked. Sarah came in first, and then, about a step behind her, came Louise. The neon lighting of the late-night eatery shouldn't have done her any favors, but I couldn't help but notice how different she looked. I punched Dawkins with more force than was necessary, and he took the hint. As rehearsed, he got up in a flamboyant show of chivalry, leaving the seat catty-corner to me open.

As Louise pulled her chair back, the waiter asked if he could get her anything. Seeming frazzled, she looked down at my empty basket and mumbled that she'd have whatever I had. Apologetically, the waiter explained that the kitchen was closed and offered her a water, and she reluctantly accepted.

"Sorry about that. I should have asked if you guys wanted me to order something for you," I said.

47

Louise smiled shyly. "It's alright; I had a hotdog at the game."

"Did you take yours well done or charred?"

"Charred," she giggled. She had her head pointed down, but her right eye was turned up toward me, and she was biting her bottom lip just a little, like she could have smiled more if she'd let herself. "It's a shame though," she continued, her grin becoming more visible as she started a gesture towards my empty basket, "I hear the chicken tender basket here is really something special."

"Oh yeah?" I questioned, casting out the bait for her to continue her monologue.

"Yeah. Sarah was telling me all about it on the way back to my house. I even promised my brothers I'd bring some home for them. They're gonna be pretty upset."

"Well, I hear—and I guess it's really just a rumor, so I'm nervous to even repeat it—but I hear that this place is open on Saturdays."

"You don't say?" She smirked with an endearing curiosity, tracking step for step with my sarcasm.

"Yeah, which works out well for you."

"How is that?" Her eyes revealing the smile she'd been trying desperately to keep hidden.

"Well, it works out well for you because tomorrow, we have a game at Rosemark, but Saturday, I'm wide open. So, if you were so inclined…"

She cut me off. "So inclined for what?" She asserted with two parts force and one part Casanova.

"What I was going to say before you so rudely interjected is that if you were so inclined, I'd be willing to bring you here before the kitchen closes."

"Oh, you'd be willing to bring me here? How endearing," she paused, adding a somewhat serious glare of disapproval before continuing, "Is that an invitation?"

"Of sorts."

A squint of the eyes and a slight shake of the head came the response.

"Can I take you out to dinner on Saturday night?" came my second attempt, a conniving grin very much visible.

"You don't even know me."

"Well, that seems like a strange reason to turn down a free dinner."

What appeared to be *an attempt* to look offended came the response.

"I'm just going to keep asking until I get an answer," I continued.

"Sure."

"Sure?" I scoffed before taking a breath and feigning deep contemplation. "I suppose there are worse responses," I continued as if pretending my words only existed in my head. "She could have said *no*. That would have been horrifying. I would've needed to leave if she had said *no*. On second thought, I was here first. I would have made her leave. Perhaps she really meant to say *no* but was scared to hurt my feelings. Surely that's what she meant by such a lame response as *sure*." I paused, turning to see the wrinkles forming on her nose as she got angry with herself for falling victim to my humor so reflexively.

"Perhaps, if we take this *sure* and we make the most of it, we could turn it into something great. Something altogether exciting. Perhaps, one day, we can receive a full, dare I say, emphatic *YES!*" I concluded, driving my fist into the air.

Gaze returning to the object of my musing, the rest of the table effectively non-existent, I resumed speaking, but this time actually addressing Louise, "I've thought it through, and I accept."

"Accept?" she asked with genuine astonishment. "Accept what? You asked *me* on the date."

Smirking but keeping an inquisitive look in my eye, I replied, "I've heard it both ways."

"You... but... that isn't...," Louise fumbled through her words in genuine confusion.

I interjected her ramblings, "I'll pick you up at seven?"

Grinning, she sat pondering, shaking her head, just slightly. "Yes." She paused to regain eye contact. "You can pick me up at seven."

Unaware of how long I'd been lost in thought, the door swinging open drove me out of my seat. Pushing the cart toward the sea of balls lying at the back of the cage, I greeted Joe. He made his way toward the lockers, putting his stuff down in no particular order before backtracking to the defunct aux cord. Operating with surgical precision, he brought the explicit thud of Eminem back to life.

Chapter 8

From my vantage point at the rear of the left-hand cage, facing the front wall of The Indoor, the wall to my right opened up to the field. Along it were three floor-to-ceiling garage doors that we'd swing open during practice to make the flow of players from field to cage smoother. And if the weather was nice, it gave the place a tropical feel.

The entry door was on the far right of the front wall. Lockers started about halfway across the room, stretching back to my left, with a dozen or so lockers making the turn, positioned along the perpendicular wall. They were a tannish gray and sat up on metal legs, leaving about a foot of open space beneath them. Stacked initially in pairs, we dismantled three of the pairs to make space for the TV centrally located in our makeshift clubhouse.

Joe meandered from the stereo back toward the entrance to The Indoor, stopping at the locker labeled "TIGER" in bold, black Sharpie on white athletic tape. He spun in the code and removed a lime green blazer that was about three sizes too wide and at least that many too long. As if donning the royal coat of arms, he dipped both hands into the sleeves and popped the jacket over his shoulders, buttoning the top front button as he spun around to face me.

"Care for an ass whoopin', Phil?" Joe opened, making a reference to Phil Mickelson's storied career, finishing second place behind Tiger Woods.

"Go fuck yourself, Eldrick," I replied, referring to Joe with Tiger's given name.

"It's another beautiful Sunday in Augusta, isn't it, Verne?" He spoke, giving his best Jim Nanz impression before replying to himself, making no attempt to change timbre, this time as the supposed voice of Verne Lundquist. "I'd say so, Jim. There's just nothing like it. Tiger and Phil making the turn for the back nine, neck and neck. You just can't draw it up any better than this."

"So, I am Phil, now?"

"Well, I've won three straight rounds, so it appears that way," Joe replied.

"Just bring the putters."

Joe met me at the tee box for our first hole, which we fondly dubbed "hole ten," given our flare for the dramatic and the fact that we only had nine makeshift styrofoam holes. By no means a birdie hole, you teed off from the rubber of the temporary mound set up in the back of the left-hand cage. The mound was probably two feet above the surrounding turf at its highest point, sloping down to about six inches at its lowest point. Covered in thick turf, controlling the speed coming off the mound was possible but not easy.

The perfect shot needed to descend off the mound and slide beneath the chair that was set up to provide an exit from inside the cage. The netting, itself, was a hazard, so if you hit it, you had to take a drop and lose a stroke. Trying to shoot the gap on your first shot was dangerous, and even if you succeeded, there wasn't much room to get the ball to check up between the start of the fairway and the netting of the right-hand cage.

With honors, coming off his previous victory, Joe had the tee box. Never one to intentionally play it safe, he lined up right at the chair and threaded the needle perfectly, his ball stopping neatly in the fairway between the two cages. Feeling the pressure but maintaining composure, I placed my ball into position and putted gently down the mound into the landing zone, not attempting perfection.

As the further player from the hole, it was immediately my turn to hit again. I navigated the breezeway provided by the legs of the chair, just to the right of Joe's ball. Pulling a quarter from the pocket of my shorts, I reached down and marked my position. Joe walked circles around his ball, stopping to examine the non-existent slope from all sorts of angles.

Getting into the hole in two was nearly impossible. The old styrofoam koozies that we'd repurposed required a precise degree of speed. A lag putt was the play, but as usual, Joe didn't lag it, pushing his second stroke about seven feet past the cup. From my position, not much closer to the hole than he had been, I took a dramatic breath before lining up and lagging mine within three inches of the foam ring. Joe gave his birdie putt a good run. It nudged the edge of the foam but ran out of steam before it could mount the inch-tall lip.

The netting wasn't really even in play as we worked our way underneath the lockers in pursuit of the seventeenth cup, but Joe managed to knick the edge of the metal leg, sending his ball careening toward the right-hand cage. An impressive bogey save kept him in the match, though, knocking him just one stroke back going into the last hole.

The easiest layout on the course, the only way to lose a stroke on eighteen was to fall apart mentally. Eleven feet of flat turf separated me from the beloved green jacket. I leaned my putter against the locker, took a long swig of Gatorade, and wiped my face and hands with a towel before consulting with my imaginary caddie.

"Crews has a chance to put this one to bed here," I narrated, advancing to the tee box. "He's executed all day. He just needs to make one... more... putt," I concluded, adding a deliberate pause between each of the last three words.

"You know, Jim," Joe interrupted, waiting until I was already standing over my ball, positioned to putt, "Crews has been in this position before, and well, I don't know another way to put it. He has just simply shit the bed." Then, turning toward his fictional co-host, he responded, "He sure has, Verne. He's always been a bed shitter."

I backed up off my ball, allowing a slight chuckle but doing my best to hide it from Joe. Collecting myself, I let out a breath and stepped back into position, looked left toward the hole, and then back down. Left again, and then back down, slid the putter back, and then followed through. Perfection. Stopping right at the front edge of the foam, I looked in Joe's direction for permission to finish out. He nodded. Not breaking stride, putter in my right hand, I knocked it into the foam ring. Giving a very gentle drive of the fist into the air, I leaned over and picked up my ball, stepping aside to give Joe the hole.

"It all comes down to this, Jim," I opened, continuing the commentary Joe had started. "Crews has done his part. A perfectly executed round. Two under. Zero bogies. The pinnacle of consistency. Now it's up to Joe. Nothing short of perfection here will force a playoff."

Slowly making his way up from a squatting position behind his ball, Joe muttered something inaudibly to himself as he stood over the ball, looking left toward the cup and then back down, left again, and then back down. He drew his putter back and then came through the ball effortlessly, sending it due east, right at the cup. He followed in close pursuit, tracking step for step with the ball. Striking the front lip of the foam, time stood still. Joe's fist began to form, the ball dropped, bounced slightly, and dropped again, right in the center of the foam ring.

"Can you believe it?!? Joe Lewis has forced the playoff!" he yelled as he made his way around the room, high-fiving the fans who had begun trickling in as we approached closer to five-thirty.

I let him have his moment of glory before cutting in, "You have the honors," I said, extending a hand toward the eighteenth tee box. "Hell of a putt."

"Thanks, Phil."

Lining up, I could tell the jitters had not fully subsided. His hands were shaking as he looked left toward the cup and then back down to his ball. After a couple more glances, he swung, sending his ball gently gliding toward the cup—a perfect lag. He tapped in for his par before tipping his cap as he threw a wave toward the side of the room devoid of any actual human fans.

I lined up, routine intact, letting out a breath, looking left at the cup, and then back down to my ball. Left again and then back down. Sliding my putter backward, I finished through the ball, coming inside it ever so slightly. Tracking at the hole, my aim must've been off slightly because the side spin was taking it right at the cup. The momentum of the collision sent the ball into the air while the foam cup followed suit, flipping through space like a deflected hockey puck. Somehow, in a miracle of physics, the foam came to a rest with my ball sitting right in the middle of it.

Bedlam ensued. I drove both hands toward the ceiling, leaning back in victory, sending my putter flying across the room. Joe dropped his head, mouth driven wide open by the disbelief erupting from within him, buried under the roar of the fans who couldn't help but echo the magnitude of the moment. Slowly, he took off the jacket and begrudgingly headed my direction.

I turned, putting my arms behind me while he threaded them into our prized possession. Taking in the crowd for a minute, I grinned emphatically. After enough of a pause to garner some boos, I turned and shook Joe's hand. Then, making my way toward the whiteboard to the right of the "TIGER" locker, I added a tally beneath my name.

My record with Louise was much more slanted than my record with Joe. He led the clubhouse series thirty-two twenty-seven, but Louise had only mustered two wins out of the forty matches we had completed. If you add in the dozen or so where she'd walked off the course mid-round, the tally was even worse.

Not much of a hand-eye athlete, Louise played an entire season of basketball in the fourth grade without scoring a single point. I asked her dad about it, and he wasn't sure she had even attempted a shot. The drive was in her, though, and she knew I loved putt-putt, so she let me help her with her set-up and teach her how to control the speed. Eventually, it clicked.

Her strategy was simple. She went for a hole-in-one every time, no matter the risk. Most rounds would fall apart after a couple of holes, and she would spend the remainder of the outing slicing aimlessly at the ball. But when she managed to snag a couple of aces, it was on.

The night that seems pertinent to this story, though, was not one of those nights. We'd gotten dinner, and I won both rounds pretty easily. The air was flat as we turned in our putters and made our way back to the truck.

After about ten minutes of silence, heading east on Houston Road, we reached a dead end. To the right, the southbound traffic took you back past the school and eventually to Johnson Road, the street both Louise and I lived off of. To the left, the northbound traffic of Walnut Road took you to the part of the county that had been built out long before developers started cutting down all the trees for cookie-cutter houses. The roads meandered between rolling hills, or at least as much *hill* as we get this close to the Mississippi Delta, with trees forming a canopy over the few cars that passed through on any given day.

When I had something on my mind, I'd drive aimlessly, roll down all the windows, and let the music make sense of my thoughts. Louise liked to go at night for the stars, but she felt too dignified to use any of the spots where other couples would park and do what high school couples do in parked cars, so it took months of thorough examination to find one of our own. It was off a road that I was pretty sure was someone's driveway, but if it was, the owner didn't seem to be bothered by us.

Every time we'd get to this intersection early on, it was a sort of litmus test for how the evening had gone. Did she want me to take a left and head toward the woods or turn right and take us south, back to her house? By this point, though, it was the summer going into my senior year, so we had been together long enough for me to hang a left without a moment's hesitation.

Pulling off the road, the silence between us rattled off the walls with nothing soft enough to deaden it. Even the roar of the crickets couldn't overcome it. Something was off. I was pretty sure I said something at dinner or on the course, but I couldn't figure out what, no matter how hard I racked my brain. I could feel in my chest that something was off. I just felt pissed. I wasn't mad at Louise, I didn't think. I wasn't sure if she was mad at me, but whatever it was, I could taste it hanging in the air of the truck. Things weren't right.

"Are you okay?" came the soft introduction from the passenger seat.

"Yeah."

"Yeah?"

"Yeah. I'm okay."

"You aren't okay," she said with a tone that probably had a lot more compassion in it than I was willing to hear.

"What do you mean *I'm not okay*?"

"I know you, Crews. You're not okay."

"Are *you* okay?" I said, turning the scrutiny in her direction.

"No."

"Well, then, why are we making this about me?" My defenses escalating with every response.

59

"I'm not okay because I can tell you're not okay."

"Well, that doesn't help anything, now does it?" I said, finally turning to see the water in her eye. "I'm sorry. I didn't mean that."

"Yeah, you did."

I gave her a puzzled look. It wasn't like me to be left without words, but this time, I couldn't find a single one.

"What the fuck is going on?" she said, her hands flying up through the tension in the air.

"What the fuck is going on?" I escalated. "You were the one pouting during dinner. And now *I* am somehow in trouble?"

"Pouting? I was pouting? Crews what?...," she paused, sidestepping my cruel words, desperate to find out what was really bothering me so much. "Did something happen?"

"No... well... I guess..." I mumbled more than said—not realizing I was stripping a layer of tension with every pause.

"What happened?"

A long silence hung in the air while I gathered the thoughts that I didn't realize were even on my mind.

"Yesterday my dad called... I mean I know *that* he called. He didn't call me. But I heard Mom talking to him," I said in a tone lacking all certainty, curious if I was answering the question she was trying to ask.

"Oh your dad who you haven't heard from in, what, five years, called and you didn't think that would be important to mention to me?" she said in an honest attempt to ease the tension with the sarcasm in her voice.

"Well, I didn't think it was a big deal."

"Well, *is* it a big deal?"

"I don't know. I guess?" I said with more of a shrug than genuine interest, turning back to distract myself with the open field in front of us.

I could hear her move toward me, and out of the corner of my eye, I saw her hand making its way onto mine. Along with it came a soft "I love you."

"I love *you*," I replied, muffled by my running nose and mounting tears. A few minutes passed before I started up again. "I know we've got a whole year before I leave, but I'm gonna leave, and it's not going to be the same. I..." Louise let the sentence hang unended in the air while I tried to find the words.

"I'm scared..," I continued. "I'm scared of what is going to happen to *this*. I'm scared that it's going to blow up or that it's just going to fade away or that somehow I am going to fuck the whole thing up. I don't know why I am scared. I don't even know what I am scared of."

There was a long silence before I heard her pull in the breath for a reply. "What isn't going to be the same?" she said with a directness that was firm in its intent but soft in its delivery.

"This… this isn't going to be the same!" I continued, "I'm gonna be off somewhere else, and I won't be here for this."

We sat there, letting the crickets take over most of the talking for at least a couple minutes before I continued. "I could stay. I could go to Rhodes. Or I could go to Southwest and play there for a year. Then we could leave together. I don't have to leave right now. I can play here and be right up the road."

"You said yesterday that you liked…" she started before I cut off her sentence.

"You're better than me." Pausing to catch my breath, she knew I wasn't finished. "You are better than me. I know you don't flaunt it. Hell, you barely even tell me about it, but I was sitting right there with your mom when the UT coach came up to her at the pool." Pausing, I turned to her stunned gaze, "I can't fucking play at UT. That's all you. They're not calling my ass," I added, letting the humor make its way through the raw emotion, adding an incoherent "I don't know" as my conclusion.

"You don't know what?"

"I can't be the reason this doesn't work."

"What does *that* mean?"

Turning to her, this time raising my voice, "I can't be the reason this doesn't work! This," I said, pointing back and forth softly at both of us, "this is the best thing I've ever had. You're the best thing I've ever had. And I'm fucking terrified that if I leave, nothing is going to be the same. And I…. I can't keep you from chasing your dreams, *either*. Because even if I stay another year, I can't play at the schools that are recruiting you. I don't even know what, I just. I..."

"*You* don't want to be the reason?" she interjected, not letting me finish. There was more vigor in her voice than I was used to. "How do you think *I* feel? You've worked your whole life for this, to have the opportunity to play where *you* want to, and now you're giving that up for *me*," she paused, and I didn't dare interrupt her. Gathering everything she had left to give, she yelled, the words seeming to come through her fingertips, "I can't be the reason you *stay* here!"

Silence.

"I guess we're kinda fucked aren't we?" I said with a dreary sort of jeer.

"Yeah I guess we are," she said, looking up at me through the wet hair of angry tears, a grin starting to work its way into position, her chest slowly coming down to earth from beating to the moon and back.

"I don't know. I don't know how it works, and I don't know how to do this. I don't have anyone to talk to about it either, and whenever I try, they tell me I shouldn't be making my decisions based on a high school girlfriend, but..."

"But what?" she interjected after I had let the thought dangle for longer than I was able to keep track of.

"I'm not fuckin' around," I said with all the resolve I could muster, this time leaving the sarcasm out of it.

A slight chuckle preceded a genuinely curious, "What?"

63

"Hell, maybe they're right. I've certainly had some bad ideas before. But this..," I paused, eyes locked into hers, "This, what we have, this is what I want. I don't know how I am supposed to do everything else, but I can't lose *this*." I was a puddle. I had felt the weight of the world on my shoulders trying to keep everything in the air.

I don't know and still don't really understand what my dad had to do with it other than the fact that he wasn't there to help. And even if he had been, I wouldn't have wanted his advice. I knew he and my mom had given up fighting with each other. There was no screaming downstairs at our house the months before he left. There was nothing. No hate. No animosity. Just nothing. When people say they fall out of love, I think that is what they mean. I think that's what I saw. They stopped being in that place together, and it didn't seem like either of them wanted to figure out how to get back. That night after putt-putt, sitting in the truck with Louise, I couldn't have put my finger on it, but I think that's what I was so scared of. I wasn't worried that Louise would stop loving *me*. I was worried she would forget how much she loved *us*. I was scared that the place where we *were* would fall apart, not all at once in something dramatic, but a little piece at a time, until there would just be nothing except some person that maybe she still loved, but not one she would fight for.

"You think I'm going to give up on this?" She said without an ounce of confusion in her voice. "Do you think I am just going to lay down and let this die?"

"No... I didn't mean that..."

Cutting me off, she launched into a monologue of her own, "You think *I'm* not scared? You think this has been easy for *me*?" Pausing to catch her breath and her composure, she started again, "Look, Crews, I fucking love *you*. And if you want to stay in Memphis, I'm not going to stop you. But you know better than to think that being a couple states away is going to change a damn thing about *this*," she concluded, crawling over the console and into my lap. I could feel her looking up at me while I stared ahead at everything that was still on my mind.

"Even if I do leave," I said, the tone of my voice comforted by the resolve in hers, "you can't come to wherever I end up. I won't let you. I can't let you pass up UT to follow me."

"You think I would be *passing up* UT?"

I didn't quite understand the question. "I'd give an arm to play at Tennessee."

"I know," she said with a pause, but whatever emotion driving it was indistinguishable.

"What do you mean, *you know*?"

"I know you'd give anything to play there. To play at the places that are recruiting me," she said, pausing for a moment. "Why do you think I don't tell you about the letters?"

"Because you love your shitty little ballplayer of a boyfriend?" I said, smiling gently through the tears.

"You aren't shitty, Crews. Watching you out there..."

"Watching me out there, what?" I interjected into her pause, impatient for her to finish, my forward gaze keeping me from seeing the emotion piling up inside her.

65

"Crews, you… That look in your eye, I can't go back to what I was doing before. If people want to think…" She kept stopping and starting as if she had never put these words together, even in her own head. "I want *that*. I don't know what my *thing* is, and I know there is more to life than baseball, but the way that it grips you. Watching you out there…. It's poetry."

I don't think she had the words for it all, but then again, she had the only word that really mattered. It *was* poetry out on that field. I had never seen it that way before, but she was right.

We have dreams, and those dreams drive us. But sometimes, we run across something that changes everything. That knocks us off track, not because it helps us think more clearly but because it changes us. That's how new dreams are born. They aren't inside us, waiting for us to find them. They are out there, and when we collide with them, we can't keep on going the way we were going before. At first, you're just playing tee ball or going on a couple dates. Sure, you like it, but it's not love. But then, somewhere along the line, nothing is the same anymore. I thought I was keeping Louise from chasing her dream, but I was wrong. I think that night, it finally became clear that her dream changed *because* of me. She didn't love to swim the way I loved baseball. She was better at it, but she didn't have the same love I did. And somehow, in colliding with me, she knew that there was poetry to be found. Not just in *me*. But *with* me. That's what people miss. People just see the part where you give up on a dream. But that's not the whole story, not when the love is real. You get a new dream. For me, baseball was still a part of it, or at least it was going to be. But for her, she was willing to take a risk that there was more out there than what she knew.

If high school relationships are different, I don't think they are different because you're young. They are different because you're blind. You haven't lived long enough to see what matters from what doesn't. But there's no guarantee that you will learn *how to see* the older you get, and there was nothing blind about Louise. She knew who I was. She knew that what we had didn't just come out of thin air. We yelled and screamed and cried and loved our way into it. Something in her knew that it didn't matter who was *right*. She just knew we couldn't *lie*. That we couldn't pretend that *okay* was enough. The fear of *it*, whatever was wrong, sitting like a monster under the bed, hanging in the flat air between us so many times, scared us more than we could fear anything else.

There was nothing in the world I cared for the way I cared for Louise, but it wasn't the sort of love that *consumed*. It gave. I was a better ballplayer. I was a better friend. I had more of my heart to give, even though it seemed like she had every ounce of it. What we had didn't just *feel* good. It *was* good.

I knew, though, even then, that what we had, if we wanted to keep it, couldn't stay the same. Not when everything around us was changing so fast. I don't know how you love something like that, that doesn't stay the same, that can't stay the same. But she did. I could see it in her eyes. She saw *me*. She saw *us*.

And she wanted every part of it.

Chapter 9

I sat down on a bench set up in our makeshift clubhouse, facing back toward the action. Coach Stephens was in the right-hand cage as the varsity guys filtered through his front-toss station like ants at a picnic, getting eight or so swings with him before rotating over to the left-hand cage for eight or so swings with Coach—a fine-tuned machine. I closed my eyes and took in a breath. It was time.

I stood up, turned toward my locker, swung open the door, unfolded my pants, slid both legs in, tucked in my jersey, and pulled the crisp, cardinal-red belt through every loop. The pants fit snug in the hips, but not too tight in the thighs. They tapered at the ankle, showing just an inch or so of the stirrups I had tucked into my low-top white cleats. The jersey had been in rotation for a few years but was still in good condition. Not a single stain. A crisp, gold block twenty-eight, framed in cardinal red, was centered on the back.

The hat was the same New Era piece the pros wear. Ours was paneled, cardinal around the back and the bill, with the front panels white to match our jerseys. It was a clean look. I pulled my Oakleys off the brim of my hat and put them into the case in my locker, gently shut the door, and headed for the exit, bat in hand.

Stepping through the garage doors facing the right field line, I could feel the warmth of the late afternoon sun sinking

68

into my perfectly smeared eye-black. The crunch of the warning track accompanied me toward the dugout, followed by the metallic click of spikes colliding with the concrete floor of the dugout as I made my way to the bat rack. Putting my bat in its customary spot, the fifth slot from the right, I doubled back toward the bench and took a seat next to my neatly positioned glove, which had remained perfectly undisturbed during the JV game.

I took in the view as the last few stragglers made their way out of The Indoor. Coach Clarke was on the three-wheeler dragging the infield while a few JV players were diligently repainting the lines and getting all the final details squared away.

Out past the group of players beginning to gather in shallow right field, I could see Sam working through each step of his pregame stretching ritual along the warning track. No one had spoken to him since he arrived.

Barely visible through the chain-link fence from my angle, I saw Biggs swing open the door to The Indoor, making his customary six-thirty entrance. The only player on the team who was allowed to show up beyond five-thirty and still play, Biggs wasn't a believer in warming up. He came to play, not to stretch.

A couple JV guys hung back to work on the infield, but most of them joined the growing mass of bodies along the right field line. Thirty-strong, we made our way out in a slow jog toward center field. Pretty small, even for a high school field, measuring 309 feet down the right field line and 311 down the left field line, I came to a rest as I punched the center of the six in the 365 marker hanging on the center field wall.

Letting the rest of the team sift past me, I took in another look at the field. Then, holding up the rear of the pack, I made my way back toward the foul line before finding my place at the center of the newly formed stretching circle. Shoulder to shoulder with Joe, we led the team through a half-hearted round of calisthenics that consisted of more shit-talking than stretching.

As the group dispersed, I flipped Joe his glove and backpedaled about twenty feet from him. Having already warmed up sufficiently from batting practice, we made abbreviated work of the long toss, pausing just enough for me to exchange some pleasantries with the opposing team in center field. Joe's throws never took my glove more than a foot or so from the center of my chest. Precision.

The park was starting to fill in, and I noticed a good number of the lawn chairs that were scattered behind home plate for the JV game were still there. The dads didn't want to miss the main event. I made my way toward the dugout and grabbed my bat, finding a spot on the warning track to continue my warmup. After a few swings, I panned the crowd and saw Louise and Mom walking from the concession stand toward the dugout. Mom reached her hand through the netting for what was more of a hold than a high five. Louise smiled at me, passing along a yellow Gatorade and a bag of peanut M&M's between the steel post of the backstop and the stone edge of the dugout.

"Your snack of champions," Louise remarked with a smirk.

"Thanks," I winked.

"Go get 'em," Mom added with a calm confidence as she walked away, headed toward her spot in the bleachers.

"What she said," Louise chimed in, pointing to Mom as she stayed put, not in any rush to head toward the student section.

About that time, I heard a crash to my left in the dugout. Coach's scowl met my gaze, the slamming of a bat having garnered the attention he was after. He looked at me and then toward where Louise was standing, but she couldn't see him, given his place behind the corner of the dugout. The artificial anger was short-lived, though, replaced by a smile as he came around the corner of the dugout, patted me on the ass and greeted Louise with a warm "Hey, sweetie" before making his way to the coaches' meeting at home plate.

The sun was still a mish-mash of setting shades as the field lights shone unnoticeably over the last few minutes of warm-ups. I turned toward the rest of the team gathered around the railing at the front of the dugout and took my place next to Dawkins.

Our announcer, Mr. Meyer, broke through the rhythm of the background music to begin the team introductions. Making short but respectable work of the opposing lineup, he gave a pause before flipping on the rising bass of the home team introduction soundtrack.

"Aaaand now for your home team starting nine! In center field, batting leadoff, number seven, Joeeeee Leeeeewisss!"

My mind found itself in another world, not hearing much about batters two through four as the timbre of "At third base, batting fifth, number twenty-eight..," made its way to my ear.

My feet moved, but I didn't feel anything beneath them. I took my place to the left of Dawkins just beyond the infield dirt as the flag caught sporadic gusts of wind from the nearly still night. It was game time.

Chapter 10

9:30 p.m.

Stadium lights reflected off the white uniforms of seniors mixed within freshmen, all treading across perfectly green grass, a porch full of rowdy idiots waiting to greet us. Caleb had a tray full of burgers and dogs scorched to hell, passing them out as if they were winning lottery tickets. I stopped and took it all in.

I veered to the right, away from the crowd, and slipped through the gate onto the path leading back toward the porch. Making her way down the steps, Louise drove her head right into my chest, taking on whatever dirt was clinging across the lettering of my jersey. As I kissed the top of her head, I felt the grip around my waist ease as she tilted back, looking for a more personal touch. I smiled and leaned my head down, delivering my second kiss as part of a combined effort that lasted longer than was probably wise given the crowd. She didn't pull away.

After making my rounds and conducting a full debrief with Caleb over a hotdog that he'd actually kept warm for me, I made my way toward The Indoor to change out of my freshly stained pants into a pair of team-issued shorts. With the dirt-brown jersey still showing my involvement in the night's victory, backpack over my right shoulder, I made my way back toward the parents who had gathered on the patio alongside the concession stand.

I greeted a couple of the parents of younger guys, thanking them for their kind words before reaching Mom and the entire Monroe clan. Mom didn't seem to be any more bothered by my odor than Louise, wrapping both arms around my waist, undeterred by the backpack.

"Good game, bud," she said softly with a proud grin.

Mr. Monroe's tilt of the head gave all the congratulations necessary.

"Big win!" Mrs. Monroe said with an excited cheer in her voice, revealing a little more emotion than the stoic she had her arm wrapped around.

"You did very good," Louise added, tapping the bill of my hat as if petting a loyal dog.

Not attempting to hide my smirk, looking toward Mr. and Mrs. Monroe, I said, "Thank you guys for coming and for sticking around. I would have come down sooner if I would have known you guys were waiting."

"Nonsense! And have you miss all that?" Mr. Monroe interjected firmly, gesturing toward the now-empty right-field porch. "We can't deprive the fans of getting to see their favorite player," he said with a sarcasm that aimed to cover his sincerity with an insult.

"You better be careful," I replied, my words dripping with a sarcasm of my own. "You keep coming to these games and staying to beg for my autograph, and they're going to make you president of the fan club."

"We'll see about that," Mr. Monroe smirked.

After swapping a few more pleasantries, Mom interjected politely, motioning us toward the parking lot while putting her arm around Louise. I stayed put as the ladies began walking toward the cars, Mr. Monroe picking up on my cue.

"So, about this curfew," I opened, in the smoothest voice I could muster.

"Midnight," he said, holding his chin in the air and gazing down his nose at me. "Not a minute past it."

"Alright, alright," I babbled, holding my hands up in surrender.

Walking shoulder to shoulder, about a foot of space between us, we didn't say another word. I knew he was looking at *her*, and he knew I was, too.

Feeling the hard-earned approval walking next to me, I thought back to the first time I'd ever gone to pick Louise up. The first time Mr. Monroe and I ever spoke.

Their house wasn't too far from mine. About five minutes up Johnson Road, back toward the deli. The house itself wasn't huge, but the lot was massive compared to mine. I remember pulling in through the gate and down a long driveway, feeling like I was picking up Rapunzel from her tower. You couldn't quite make out the house from the street, so even though I'd passed it thousands of times growing up, I'd never gotten a real look at it. As I closed in, the driveway split, leading toward a three-car garage on the right and a circle drive toward the left. Coming nearly to a stop, I turned toward the right. The cream-colored brick had a unique texture, accented by the ivy-draped columns that framed a covered walkway connecting the garage to a modest but charming home.

Putting my truck in reverse, I backed into a cutout along the circle drive, bordered by a three-foot-high brick retaining wall. Each detail of the hardscape was meticulously designed, with the cap of the wall matching the blue-gray stone defining the perimeter of the meandering driveway stretching back toward the road.

I surveyed the immaculate yard; not a single blade of pristine grass out of place. After one final sweep of anything that seemed out of place inside my truck, I let out a breath and stepped toward the house.

Walking up slowly, my heart ringing in my ears, I began to debate which would be more chivalrous: to ring the doorbell or knock on the door. The wrought iron pattern on the storm door proved too much of a barrier, so I opted for the doorbell. Pressing the button firmly, I stepped back. Examining the door from top to bottom at least a dozen times, no one seemed to be in a hurry to let me in. Deciding it best to just work on my patience, I stood there thumbing my pockets until the door finally swung open.

"Hey, come in!" came the warm greeting from the smile I had been waiting all day to see.

Wiping my boots with decent vigor on the welcome mat, hoping there wasn't too much mud still clinging to the leather sole, I stepped in. The house was laid out where you could see about half the living room from the front door, but you had to walk a couple more steps in order to see around the corner to where Mr. Monroe was sitting.

I wasn't quite sure how much eye contact was wise, so I took in a view of the backyard as I made my way to him. The house cast a shadow, but it was still light enough to see a patio that stretched the entire width of the living room's floor-to-ceiling windows.

A brick paver walkway led from the patio toward the pool. My eyes worked back and forth as I did the math in my head. The pool had to be at least thirty yards long. I could feel my mouth slipping open in amazement as Mr. Monroe started, "You a swimmer, son?" A puzzled look on my face must've encouraged him to continue. "You seem pretty interested in the pool."

"I, uh, I've never seen anything like that. It's pretty impressive."

"Well, Louise likes to swim, and I like to keep my eye on her. So this works out well for everybody," Mr. Monroe added with a smirk, making it abundantly clear who was in charge.

"Smart man," I replied, extending my hand to meet his. "I'm Crews."

He returned the greeting, delivering a firm but not overpowering handshake. As our hands returned to their respective sides, I saw him give a look to Louise. Without hesitation, she grinned at him, turned to me, and let me know that she needed to *finish getting ready*. My eyes must have given away my nerves because I could tell Mr. Monroe was getting a laugh at my expense as he ushered me out the sliding glass door and onto the patio.

"Can I get you something to drink?" he offered, motioning to the stone counter built into the far side of the patio.

"Sure, I uh… I'll take a water if you have one."

I sat there feigning confidence and pretending my heart rate was normal while Mr. Monroe mixed up a fresh cocktail. He returned with a clear bottle in one hand and a lime wedge dropped atop something that appeared to be much stronger in the other. He handed me the bottle and took his seat, lifting the glass up past his beard and taking a sip that made short work of whatever he had taken so long to make. "So you like my daughter," he stated more than asked.

The words hanging in the air, I could feel his gaze turning toward me. Set up not quite facing each other, I turned my head slightly to look him in the eye. "To be honest, sir, I don't really even know your daughter. I uh... I know *about* her, and I've wanted to ask her out for a long time now, but I really don't *know* her. I guess I am sitting *here* because I'd like to get to know her."

The emotion finally became distinguishable in his eyes; his response was brief and to the point. "Good."

Without feeling a need to add anything more to our discussion, I took a swig of water, thrown off by the carbonation hidden behind the yellow label that must have come with them from Texas. I crossed my right leg over my left and savored my first real breath since coming outside.

A few months later, sometime around the start of the summer, going into junior year, we found ourselves back on the porch. Mr. Monroe had given Louise that same look, and she had gone up to do the same imaginary routine of getting ready. In our silent ritual, I settled into the same Adirondack chair overlooking the pool as he took a seat across from me. This time, there was no intro from his side of the patio. He knew it was my turn to speak, and I knew he was waiting.

"I'm crazy about your daughter," came my opening line, shot like a roman candle into the warm, humid air.

"You going to look after her?" He replied, letting the words hang in the space between us before turning his eyes to meet mine.

"Yes, sir," I replied with more bravado than I had ever directed at him.

"Good," he said, adding a different kind of pause this time —one that indicated he had more to offer. "The way that she looks at you…," he continued, a tinge of shakiness in his tone, "She trusts you." He paused, turning to look me in the eye, "It's my job to *not* trust you. You know what I mean, son?"

"Yes, sir."

"But she trusts you. And she's a smart young woman," he paused, "Don't fuck that up."

Chapter 11

10:00 p.m.

Mom and I walked slowly as we closed the last few steps toward her car, her right arm wrapped around my waist. The temperature had dropped since first pitch, and she had added an additional layer to compensate—a blanket she'd sewn from all my old travel-ball tee shirts. Tiger logos stitched across graphics from tournaments we'd won all over the southeast, from Knoxville to Texarkana. It was a fan favorite amongst the other moms. As I leaned forward to open the driver-side door, she handed me the blanket and slid down into her seat. I ran my thumbs across a faded tee shirt with green script—*Rumble on the River - May 12-14, 2006 - Marion, Arkansas*—the weekend I hit my first homerun. Folding it up, I pulled open the back left door and tossed it in gently before stepping back to see her off. "Be careful tonight, bud," she said, her maternal instinct looking right through me.

"I will," I said before shutting her door and turning back toward Louise.

I could tell the Monroes were still talking as I sauntered back in their direction, but it was too soft for me to make out what they were saying until Mr. Monroe turned his attention toward me. "Midnight," he said as he backed toward the driver-side door of his truck, repeating his ruling one last time, this time with a wink. "Midnight." Mrs. Monroe gave a slight wave and blew a kiss to Louise as she climbed up into the passenger seat.

80

Making our way back to where I had parked, I put my arm around Louise, pulling her head in toward my chest. She got a firm grip of me with one hand while she took a long look at the fictional watch on the other, "Well, we waited too long to get Hueys. If my memory serves, which it always does, their kitchen closes at ten."

"Poor planning on my part," I said with an exaggerated degree of remorse.

"Did you get enough to eat out there?" she asked, tilting her head back toward the field. "Or do you need something else before we go to Dawkins'?"

"Yeah, I probably need to grab something. How does Micky D's sound?"

"Sarah and I ate before the game, so I'm good," she responded, bringing her free arm in to complete the loop around my waist, giving me a squeeze before continuing in a tone as if I were her five-year-old son, "We can get some Micky D's for my little slugger, though."

Savoring every bite of my two McDoubles and large fry from the passenger seat, we pulled onto Dawkins' street a little before ten-thirty. Parking a few houses down, a decent supply of trucks lined the curbs in both directions. I chuckled at the complete lack of discretion. There was no attempt to hide what was going on.

The street was dead quiet, though. We knew we could only get away with such a blatant gathering if we let all the neighbors go to bed at a reasonable hour. You don't get the cops called for drinking. You get the cops called for making too much noise, and then they arrest you for drinking. One of those things they don't teach you in class, but we'd managed to learn early on.

Strolling up along the right side of the house, we passed through the back gate. The pool's water lay perfectly still. Soft blue lighting reflected off the walls that lifted out of the water toward a gray polished concrete edge, a faint hint of steam making its way up through the cool air. After a few steps, we could see into the house. Not packed, but at least a few dozen kids. It was bigger than our normal crowd.

As I reached out to open the back door, I almost fell over as the shock of the locked handle jolted my momentum. While I attempted to gather my composure, Louise got a good chuckle in at me. I could tell she was looking over my shoulder through the glass door, so I turned, curious what she knew that I didn't. Looking in, I saw Dawkins run around the counter from the kitchen into the laundry room before emerging a few seconds later with something on a platter.

As I brought my hand up to knock out the glare cast across the glass, I saw Joe reach in toward the door and flip the lock. I grabbed the handle, this time with more success, and stepped back to let Louise go in as the roar of a horrendously choreographed rendition of *Happy Birthday* erupted.

I looked over at Louise, who had already managed to slip a party hat around her head and was standing with her hands together just under her chin, giving me one of those looks a golden retriever gives you when they drop a tennis ball at your feet. Leaning over to blow out my candles, I heard the whisper of "Happy birthday, baby" in my ear as she delivered a gentle kiss to my eye-black-stained cheek.

"Thank you," I said softly, tilting my head down toward her before lifting my gaze up to address the crowd. "Wonderful execution, Dawkins. I didn't know you had it in you."

Dawkins, still holding the cake on a platter that was far nicer than his mom would have allowed us to use for such an occasion, began, "Technically, we still have another hour or so, but Sarah said that the curfew extension wasn't granted, so we had to move up the festivities slightly." Turning to clear beer cans off the island at the center of the kitchen, he sat the platter down quite dramatically before addressing Louise with a steak knife in hand. "Care to do the honors?"

"Gladly," she replied with a grin and a royal bow, taking the knife in her hand.

Leaning up against the frame of the doorway, I watched as Louise made her way across the cake, delicately slicing perfectly even pieces and putting each of them onto little plates. She had orchestrated the whole thing: the cake, the plates, the little hats, hell, even the chorus of *Happy Birthday*. And she'd managed to explain the plan in terms that *Dawkins* could execute on. I'm sure Sarah provided some helpful leverage, but still, convincing Dawkins to execute on anything more complicated than a bunt coverage was impressive.

After handing out pieces to the mob that had immediately surrounded her, I saw Louise cut an unusually large piece from the far corner. Spinning backward, she opened up the freezer, pulled out a pint of ice cream, and plopped an extra large scoop of vanilla onto the plate. Holding the plate with both hands, spoon in her mouth, she brought her hips right up to mine, leaning back just enough to make room for the plate.

"Happy birthday," she mumbled almost indistinguishably, a grin emerging from either side of the plastic spoon.

Wrapping my left arm around her, I leaned down to kiss her cheek, catching a glimpse of her nearly microscopic masterpiece: up in the corner, across the white cream cheese finish, was a tiny red heart.

"Where did you get this?" I said as if genuinely curious for the answer.

A smirk accompanied her firm response. "I made it, silly."

"Hmmm. How about that?" I said in mock disbelief. "It's not terrible," I added with a slight frown and a nod of my head. Unsatisfied with my review, she stood there, staring me down, waiting for me to finish. "The frosting," I continued, adding a dramatic pause to build the suspense, "It's like you knew that carrot cake was my favorite. Did Joe tell you? How could you have possibly known?" I lifted the plate above her head as she moved in for another hug, "It's the best," I concluded. "Thank you."

"You're welcome," came the whispered response, more into my chest than directed at me.

About the moment her words hit my ear, the blur of a white flying object drove my left hand off her back and into the air just in time to greet a cold Miller Lite generously provided to me by Doug on the opposite side of the room. It wasn't exactly the pairing you'd find at a Parisian bistro, but the light finish of the American pilsner hit the spot just fine.

As I looked around the room, the size of the crowd threw me off. I was used to some small get-togethers, but this was a full-scale party. I recognized everyone's face, but there were definitely a couple people there who got their invitation through the grapevine. I laughed at the handful of freshmen I saw huddled in the corner, thinking about how much work must have gone into their schemes. As you get closer to graduation, parents seem to think that taking your story at face value will keep the peace better, but at fifteen, you really have to put effort into the lies.

Louise was leaning up against the counter next to me, enjoying a piece of the cake she'd put so much love into. And I know I sat there for a while and talked with her, but I don't really remember what about. I mostly remember how I never liked to leave her hanging in settings like that. Not because she couldn't handle herself—she was plenty personable—but because the crowd didn't mean anything to her. The way she saw it, *I* was her person, so she didn't put much stock in being admired by anyone else. She knew I liked to work the crowd a little bit, though, especially after a big win, so when Joe found himself in need of a playing partner, I knew she wasn't going to let me turn him down.

After stringing together a pretty dominant run, I let one of the younger guys sub in for me while I made my way across the room to find Louise. "I'm not saying we need to get home by exactly midnight," I started with a smirk, "but I don't want to be *too* late, you know?"

"Eh, I think this may actually be the one night that your dimples get you some grace from Dad," she said with a confident shrug of the shoulders. "Why don't you go play another game or two?" she continued, pointing to the folding table I had just left. "I'm hearing rumors that Dawkins is going to let us get in the pool later."

"You'd get in the pool?" I said with genuine curiosity.

"What do you mean, *would I get in the pool?*" she responded back with equal curiosity.

"Unless I missed you throw a bag in my car, I don't see any swimsuit, and little Miss Rule Follower doesn't normally just go around jumping into pools with a bunch of baseball players without any clothes on."

"Go back to your table, Mister Rule Breaker. Don't you worry about me."

Hands going up in mock surrender, I returned to my position alongside Joe. Our dominance continued for a couple more games but came to an abrupt halt when Doug finally recruited Sam to play. They, or more accurately, Sam, made quick work of us.

The sting of defeat was short-lived, though, as the streak of Dawkins' caramel skin flying past the window toward the pool brought me right back to life. I turned my gaze back toward the kitchen and locked eyes with Louise. She gave a shrug of the shoulders and a conniving smile before ripping off her sweatshirt.

The flow of brunette hair framed the shoulders of the most beautiful thing I'd ever laid eyes on. Her sports bra, pulled tight across her chest, painted a picture that left less for the imagination than was usual in a setting like this. I started toward her, eyes locked. As she ran her hands through her hair, the slight pop of her biceps revealed the athlete that she made no attempt to hide. My gaze made its way down, exploring the abs that came so effortlessly, framed by the soft curve of her hips. She bent forward, dropping the sweatpants she'd borrowed from me toward the floor, but kept her eyes right on me. The soft lighting of the kitchen reflected off legs that looked longer than her height allowed them to be. She stepped both feet out and gave a slight turn, looked over her shoulder at me, and tilted her head gently toward the door, inviting me in.

Without anything by way of rebuttal, I followed my orders to a tee, covering the distance between myself and the pool in as few steps as possible, shedding everything but my sliding shorts in a far less enticing rhythm, culminating my pursuit with a cannonball entry. I came up for air, turned both directions, and, not seeing her, backed up to rest my arms atop the concrete edge.

A blur of fair skin made its way toward me beneath the surface as she wrapped her arms around my legs, slowly pulling herself up. I can still see her. Head lifting out of the water, those warm, hazel eyes looking right into mine as she pressed her chest against me, guiding my hands in a direction I had no objection to.

"You sure you want to get me home by midnight?" she whispered, taking a small bite with her as she made her way back down my chest.

Heart pounding, I dropped my lips down to meet hers, the taste of saltwater solidifying our plans.

Chapter 12

Not much of what came out of the juror's mouth made its way to my ear. I knew what they would find. Perhaps they spent a couple of hours arguing over the details here and there. *This* charge over *that* charge, but there wasn't much to be made out of the difference.

I'd watched the judge for that entire month, and he'd watched me. He'd heard stories, but he wasn't there. He wasn't there in Mr. Winchester's field. He wasn't there on the porch with me and Mr. Monroe. He hadn't been there in the cafeteria watching me catch Louise. He wasn't there all the days I did get Louise home safe. He wasn't there *that* day. Not at the game. Not at Dawkins'. He saw the pictures of the crash, but they didn't tell the story that I knew he knew.

He knew I wasn't driving the truck that night. The jury didn't see it, the Monroes didn't see it, Mom didn't see it, but I knew the Judge could see. It didn't matter why, but he knew I was in the passenger seat. He knew that whatever caused Louise to swerve into the rumble strip and then back across into the southbound lane, right as Jack and Morgan Beale happened to be there—was my fault. And he knew that the fault lay at a depth far below the story—deeper than just what happened.

Sitting there looking up at him, he wasn't angry like he had been the first few days. I hadn't spoken a word to him, but he knew all he needed to know about me. He knew what I wanted, and I knew he would give it to me.

There was no appeal. I got up and walked out of the courtroom with the only thing I had left.

People say they believe in forgiveness, but I don't believe *them*. It's not that they are lying. I think they mean it when they say it, but they don't know *what* they are saying. I think what they *mean* is that they know it could have been them. They mean that they know they've made some mistakes, too, and that they are lucky to have not been in that place where I was. But I don't think that's forgiveness. You may be able to understand how I got there, how what I did wasn't so bad. Maybe you read this, and you don't think I'm evil. Just a kid in the wrong place at the wrong time. Maybe you think that I learned my lesson from the first time. That somehow handing the keys to Louise gets me off the hook. But you weren't there with me and Mr. Monroe after the game. You didn't see the look in his eyes. He knew what I was. He'd been me, too, once. He believed me when I told him that night that I'd get her home safe. He knew we wouldn't make curfew. But he believed *in* me.

If there hadn't been a car headed south that night, Louise might still be here. But the Beales were there that night, headed south. And I can't blame them. I don't even know them. There is nothing about them in these pages. They were only in my life long enough for my truck to send them crashing into a lake. But the weight of them is still here, and it's different than the weight of Louise. I took something away that I didn't even know. I know what it is like *to love*, but I don't know what it was like to love Jack and Morgan Beale. I know what it is like to lose someone you love, but I don't know what it is like to lose *them*. All that pain and horror, the memories that never got a chance to be made, all that weight and loss has to land somewhere.

And if I can't put it on me, then I don't know where to put it. I've tried to blame the world. To blame fate for putting all of us there at that moment. But if that is the case, if fate drove us to do the things we did, then no one has the right to put any of us in *here*, within these walls.

If it is all fate, then there's no living. And that can't be. There wouldn't be any poetry in that. I lived. Louise lived. The failing, the fighting, the screaming, the loving—it matters so much that we can't even understand it. It is so real that we can't write *it*. We can only write *about* it.

I don't know what all this says about me, but I don't think it matters. Louise didn't make it home. I didn't protect her. So, I've gotten what I deserve. The part of me that could move from the past and into the future died with them that night. I knew that then, and I know it now. I don't want the jury to hate the world for putting us in the wrong place at the wrong time. I put us there.

Maybe, reading this, you *can* see the fountain after all. Maybe *I'm* the one who can't. Maybe I'm the one wandering in from the desert. Maybe you can see the pain and the beauty. The love and the loss. But even if you saw the most gruesome part. Even if you could have been there when Louise and I left Dawkins, driving right by her house and up Walnut Road to find our hideaway, already two hours late for curfew. Even if you'd seen her reach over the console, tires rolling full steam ahead, mad that I hadn't put my own seatbelt on when she'd asked. Even if you'd heard the hum of the rumble strip, the screech of the wheels in a leftward jolt, and the impact—the deafening roar of the impact. Even if you'd felt the haze of unconsciousness, the burn of hot asphalt, the chaos of the mangled metal. Even if you smelt it—air steeped in death. Even if you saw her lying there, breathless and still, flesh split open by the crack of windshield glass, her bones slouched unnaturally around the base of a tree. Even if you'd run up alongside me to hold her. To scream. To fight God in the cool of the morning.

You still wouldn't know the thirst. You wouldn't feel the hunger. You wouldn't understand how telling the truth of what happened wouldn't keep me from having to bear the cost of what died that night.

And I guess now, finally, I'm not mad that you can't know that. That you can't feel that. If you could, then it wouldn't be mine.

Chapter 13

The guard, Gary, who watches the door closest to the officer's courtyard has a kid who plays ball. Not sure he's a ballplayer yet, but if he starts taking my advice, maybe he can end up good enough to play behind someone like Sam one day. He's got a swing that starts a little too closed, so he's always pulling his foot out, losing his front hip, and causing his eyes to change plane.

Officer Gary gets frustrated when he pops out to the second baseman so much, complaining that he's told him a million times to keep his feet still. Dads don't realize, though, that it's not so much your feet that cause you to miss the ball. Watch a pro game, and guys have their feet set up in all sorts of ways. Chipper tapped, and guys when I played would bring their front foot up damn near their hip. It's not the motion that kills you. It's when it gets out of sync. It's when the swing loses its rhythm. That's when you pop out to the second baseman.

I think Gary could know that if he wanted to. He could help his son find a rhythm—help him get a little more comfortable and teach him how to keep his eyes on plane. But I don't think that's what he's mad about, really. I think he's mad that his kid's not Sam. He sees that he could be, that somewhere in him is the ability to be great. He's mad about what those pop-outs say about his kid's nature. He's mad that his kid wasn't just born a ballplayer. And I guess, in some way, I don't blame him. There is something that seems unfair about guys like Sam—not that they don't work hard, but that no matter how hard guys like Gary's son work, they'll never be as good as Sam. They'll always fall short.

Maybe I am wrong. Maybe that isn't why Gary is mad, but I only say it about *him* because I know it was true about *me*. I was scared that because writing *this* came so hard, I might not be cut out for writing in the first place. And that cut off my air. I didn't want to find some other way to live up to *it*. I knew that what the other guys had, tucked away on those little slips of paper behind the counter in the library, was in me, but I couldn't get it out. I couldn't stop reading, either, but the more I read, the angrier I got. Each poem sat there looking down at me—strangling me with a judicious contempt.

And then, somewhere along the line, I was *there*. Not all the way there *with* her, but so damn close I thought I could touch her. Somehow, in the trying and the failing, in the erasing and the rewriting, from the start until now, I'm closer than where I was. And just being close, I know I can't do anything else.

But for *that* to be, *these words* can't be for anybody else.

So I'll have to leave the library here in a little while. I'll find Gary over by the officer's courtyard, and he'll hand me my customary cigarette. I'll lean in, back to the camera in the corner of the hall, and let him light me up. He'll swing open the door, and I'll step out onto the courtyard. After a nice long drag, I'll make a little fire with this paper.

And while it burns, I'll read what I can one last time.

93

Love on high
Love on high

Who to bring it down but I

This solemn vow
No way but down

Not that the high has ceased

This place yet not
Lest above

Some may roam

Until these shackles
One might drown

Here my freedom lies

Not in the open skies
But with these pains

I know are mine.

the end

Author's Note

As I have drawn closer to completing the version of this story that you hold in your hands, the magnitude of the truths hidden within has become so great that I fear I will never be able to do them justice. Their roots lie far too deep for my prose to tread. It is as if I have begun a story I could never possibly complete.

My hope, though, remains. I believe I have told the story the way Crews *could have* told it.

And that seems to me like something worth doing.

Acknowledgements

To my family: For supporting me, raising me, and showing me what it is like to be loved. Thank you.

To my teammates: For the friendship and the putt-putt matches. Thank you.

To my coaches: For taking the time to make me into a ballplayer—on and off the field. Thank you.

To my teachers: For pushing me even when I was uninterested in being pushed. Thank you.